CHEATING THE FUTURE PAST FOR THE 2

BY: CHENELL PARKER

Previously on Cheating the Future for the Past Part 1

"Rich, baby, please answer the phone," Anaya begged for the fifth time in less than an hour.

She'd been calling him for two days straight and he hadn't answered any of her calls. They were supposed to spend a few days together since her girls were with Tigga, but Rich had been avoiding her. He wanted them to spend time at her house, but Anaya suggested that they get a room. She had just started working at their local dollar store, so she even offered to pay for it. Instead of being happy about their plans, Rich went off on her. One month of separation from Tigga had turned into two and nothing between her and Rich had changed. Anaya still wouldn't let him come to the house and he was done playing the same game with her. She thought for sure that he would have come around by now, but he was still ignoring her. Tigga had dropped the girls off home the night before and Rich was still nowhere to be found.

"Mama, can we have some ice cream?" Anaya's oldest daughter, Tia, asked when she walked into the living room.

"Okay baby," Anaya answered.

"She said okay!" Tia yelled to her other sisters. She was about to run back into the other room before Anaya stopped her.

"Who was at your daddy's house when y'all were over there?" Anaya asked her daughter.

"Nobody," Tia replied, just like always.

"He didn't have a lady friend over there or nothing?" she continued to pry.

"No, but he talked on the phone with her," Tia said, making

her mother's heart skip a beat.

"With who? What's her name?"

"I don't know, but my daddy said that we're going to see her soon," Tia replied.

"Has she ever been there when y'all were there?" Anaya asked.

"No, but she got clothes and stuff in my daddy's closet. And my daddy let us use some of her soap that was in the bathroom," Tia revealed before she walked away.

Anaya was happy when she left because the tears fell as soon as she did. Her mother was right. Tigga broke up with her and moved out to be with somebody else. That hurt more than anything, especially after she did so much to try to keep him there. She did Rich dirty behind a nigga who didn't even give a fuck about her. She knew, without a doubt, that Tigga had loved her once before, but he seemed to have no feelings for her at all anymore. And if that wasn't bad enough, thoughts of Rich being with somebody else were starting to drive her crazy as well. Picking up her phone once again, Anaya decided to give her best friend Erica another call.

"That bastard still didn't answer the phone for you?" Erica asked when she picked up.

"Nope," Anaya sighed in defeat.

"His ass is right outside. I just told him that you were looking for him," Erica replied.

"And what did he say?" Anaya questioned.

"He didn't say anything. He just walked outside and started talking to his friends."

"That nigga must take me to play with. I'm about to put some clothes on and come over there. He can't ignore me if I'm right up in his face," Anaya snapped in anger.

"Come on through girl. I'll be home," Erica said.

Anaya was about to reply, until she heard her daughter's screaming in the other room.

"Mama! Something is wrong with Amari!" Tia yelled.

"She's shaking!" Talia screamed.

Anaya jumped up from the sofa and ran into the room with the phone still glued to her ear.

"Oh my God! Amari!" she yelled frantically when she saw her baby girl on the bedroom floor shaking violently.

"What's wrong Anaya?" Erica yelled.

"Send an ambulance to my house Erica. My baby is having a seizure!" Anaya yelled.

Her other girls were crying hysterically, as she led them out of the room and into the living room. Once Amari stopped shaking, Anaya laid her on her side, just like she'd been instructed to do once before. She was able to breathe a little easier when Erica sent her a text, telling her that an ambulance was in route to her house and so was she. She covered her baby girl up with a blanket and immediately dialed Tigga's number to let him know what was going on. When she got his voicemail three times in a row, she dialed Tessa's number and prayed that she would answer.

***

"Are you mad?" Keller asked while looking across the table at Tigga.

They were out eating dinner at one of her favorite soul food restaurants, when she hit him with some bullshit about getting her own apartment. Keller loved that she could talk to Tigga about anything without reservations. Unlike Leo, he asked her what she wanted to do, instead of telling her what she was going to do. He valued her opinion and that meant a lot.

"Nah, I'm not mad; I'm pissed," Tigga replied.

"But why?" Keller asked, like she didn't already know.

"You're not making sense to me right now Keller. Why would you go spend money to rent an apartment, when I've offered to let you stay with me for as long as you want to?"

"I know Tigga, but I need to be settled. I have clothes at four different houses and that just don't make sense," Keller replied.

Aside from his house, Keller had belongings by Kia, Tessa, and Mo's houses. She divided her time up with all four of them, but she was with Tigga the most.

"That's your fault though Keller. My girls already know you. That was your decision to leave and go sleep somewhere else when they come over there. You think I give a fuck if they tell Anaya anything? She gon' find out sooner or later anyway. That shit don't make a bit of sense," Tigga argued.

"I didn't bring it up to start an argument. I just wanted to know how you felt about it," Keller replied.

"I don't want to argue with you either baby, but I don't agree with you getting your own apartment. You just told me not too long ago that you be scared and nervous when you're by yourself. Why would you want to get an apartment that you'll probably never sleep in?" Tigga questioned.

Keller looked away because she knew that he was right. She would probably be paying rent in a place that she would hardly ever sleep in. But she didn't want to smother Tigga by being in his space all the time either. He said that he loved her being around, but she wasn't so sure.

"Look at me, Keller," Tigga said as he gently turned her head back around to face him. "Now, tell me what's really going on?"

"You would tell me if you needed your space, wouldn't you?" Keller questioned.

"You can't be serious right now," Tigga replied while grabbing her hand.

"You know how I am Tigga. I just have to be sure," Keller said.

"You need to stop with all the doubts Keller. I agree, we did move fast, but you can't put a timer on everything. It's not like we just met. We just decided to be in a relationship. I'm almost thirty years old and I don't have time for the games. I need to know right here, right now. Are you with me or not?" Tigga asked while looking her in her eyes.

"I'm with you, baby," Keller said, making him smile.

"Cool, so that means no more sleeping out when my girls come over. That's your house too and you don't have to ever leave it if you don't want to," Tigga replied.

"Okay." Keller smiled.

"Maybe now you can start claiming me as your man," Tigga teased her.

"I always claim you as my man," Keller replied, right as his phone started ringing.

When Tigga looked at his phone and saw that it was Anaya, he declined her call and gave Keller his undivided attention once again. Anaya had been calling him all night and he didn't have time to be arguing with her.

"You can answer it baby," Keller said when the phone buzzed on the table a few seconds later.

"I'm good. I don't have time for Anaya and her bullshit. She's always calling for dumb shit just to piss me off. Her stupid ass called me for some washing liquid the other day," Tigga said, making Keller laugh.

"Stop lying," Keller chuckled, right as her phone started ringing, displaying Tessa's phone number. She answered with a huge smile on her face, but it disappeared when Tessa started talking.

"What's wrong?" Tigga asked when he saw Keller's facial expression.

"Okay Tessa, I'll tell him right now," Keller said right before she hung up the phone.

"What happened?" Tigga questioned.

"Tessa said that Amari just got rushed to the hospital. She had a seizure," Keller replied, while giving him all the details that Tessa had just given her.

"Shit!" Tigga yelled as he jumped up from the table.

He reached into his pocket and pulled out some money and threw it on the table. Keller grabbed her purse and was right behind him, as he rushed out of the front door and headed to his car. They were about twenty minutes away from children's hospital, so Tigga wasted no time making his way over there. Keller could tell that he was nervous and she understood why. Tigga ran red lights and stop signs trying to get to his destination. Keller not only prayed for Amari's health, she also prayed for them to get there in one piece as well. She was happy when they finally pulled up to the hospital and parked in the visitor's parking lot.

"You want me to wait downstairs for you?" Keller asked, once they walked through the front doors.

"No, come on," Tigga replied as he grabbed her hand and walked up to the nurse's station.

After getting Amari's room number, they got onto the elevator and made their way to her room. Amari's room was at the end of the hall, but Tigga could see a few people standing outside of the room as they walked in that direction. Donna was the first person to look his way and she was pissed when she saw Keller walking up with him. She remembered Keller's face from seeing them out at the restaurant not too long ago. Before Tigga could utter one word, Anaya stepped out of the room and rushed right over to him.

"What the fuck is this bitch doing here with you?" Anaya yelled while pointing to Keller.

"Where is my daughter?" Tigga asked while tightening his grip around Keller's waist.

"Don't worry about where she is. Answer my fucking question!" Anaya yelled.

"Calm down Naya," one of her auntie's said, as she walked over and rubbed her back.

"Fuck that! This bitch got me all the way fucked up right now. I knew something was up with y'all when we went to Florida!" Anaya continued to yell.

"That's enough Anaya. Security is gonna throw all of us out here if you don't stop screaming!" her mother yelled.

"I don't give a fuck! He's a disrespectful ass nigga for even bringing that hoe here."

Tigga wasn't in the mood to deal with Anaya's stupid ass at the moment, so he just ignored her. Keller didn't seem fazed by her ranting either, but that didn't stop her from going off. He was happy when he saw Tessa and his mother walking down the hall and he was sure that Keller was too.

"Bitch, I know you knew about this too. You're probably the one who hooked them up!" Anaya screamed at Tessa as soon as she and Christy walked up.

"How is Amari?" Tessa asked, while ignoring Anaya. It wasn't the time for pettiness and it definitely wasn't the place.

"I don't even know. She's too busy acting a fool to tell me anything," Tigga answered.

"Where are the other girls?" Christy asked to no one in particular.

"Erica picked them up and took them home with her," one of Anaya's aunties spoke up.

"Y'all can leave. I don't want you here to see my baby with that bitch. I'm calling security!" Anaya yelled.

"What's going on with Amari?" Christy asked.

"I don't know nothing ma. I just got here too," Tigga replied in aggravation.

Anaya was serious about calling security and they assured her that they were on their way up. When the elevator down the hall chimed a few minutes later, she was happy when she saw two officers step out and head down the hall towards them.

"What's going on? Is there a problem?" one of the officers asked as soon as he walked up to them.

"No officer, everything is fine," Christy replied.

"Everything is not fine. I am the mother of the patient and I want them gone," Anaya said, pointing at Tigga and Keller.

"Why are you doing this Anaya? You should be ashamed of yourself," Christy fussed.

"Fuck all that dumb shit! Where is my daughter? That's all that I'm concerned about right now," Tigga yelled angrily, making people come out of their rooms to see what was going on.

"You need to calm down sir. This is a hospital and there are other patients on this floor. I can't have all of y'all standing in the hallway like this. I'll let the parents and the grandparent's stay. Everybody else needs to go to the waiting room," the officer informed them.

Anaya was heated when she saw Tigga whispering something in Keller's ear. She almost lost it when he bent down and kissed Keller on the lips, right before she and Tessa walked away. Anaya's aunts and cousin followed behind them, but they bypassed the waiting room and went outside instead. That left Tigga and Christy alone with Anaya and her mother. Security hung around, just to make sure everybody stayed calm.

"Can I see my daughter now?" Tigga asked calmly, right as the elevator down the hall chimed once again.

"Awe shit," Donna mumbled loud enough for everyone to hear.

Everyone looked in the direction of the man and woman who were walking towards them, but not everyone knew who they were. Anaya's heart started beating fast and her palms were sweating like crazy when she saw Rich and his mother walking in their direction. As bad as she wanted to see him earlier, she wished he would just disappear right now. Talking to Tigga about anything was out of the question at the moment. She was heartbroken when she saw him walk up with Keller, but she still wasn't ready for him to find out about Rich.

"Rich, let me talk to you for a minute," Donna said, trying to lead her daughter's past mistake back down the hall.

"Nah, we don't have nothing to talk about. What's up Anaya?" he said while looking over at her.

"Nothing is up," Anaya replied in almost a whisper.

"So you've been trying to call me all day about nothing?" Rich questioned with a scowl on his face.

He knew without a doubt who Tigga was, but he didn't know by looking at his pictures that he was so tall and buffed. Rich was pretty tall himself, but he was damn near looking up to Tigga. The nigga's look screamed money, which made Rich even more intimidated by him. Just by looking at him, he could see why Anaya chose Tigga over him. He was fooling himself thinking that he could compete with the other man and he was done trying. He knew that the other woman standing there with him was his mother because Anaya had pointed her out to him on several occasions.

"We'll talk later Rich. This is not a good time," Anaya mumbled nervously.

"Y'all can do this on your own time. I need to go see about Amari," Tigga said as he and Christy walked over to the hospital room door.

"This is not the time or the place Rich. Just leave and let Anaya call you later," Donna suggested.

"I'm not going nowhere!" Rich yelled in anger.

"Keep it down sir," one of the security guards warned. "Now, y'all can either leave or go sit in the waiting room down hall. Only the parents and grandparents are allowed back here right now."

"Cool, then we're in the right place," Rich replied, making Anaya cringe.

"And what is that supposed to mean?" Christy questioned him with her hands on her hips.

"It means that you and your son can leave. Amari is my daughter and her granddaughter," Rich replied smugly, while pointing to his mother.

Chapter 1

Tigga stopped in his tracks and turned to face the man that he now knew as Rich. That was his first time ever seeing him, but he was sure that he would never forget his face.

"The fuck did you just say nigga?" Tigga asked as he approached the other man.

The security guards were standing right there, but they looked to be waiting for Rich to answer the question, just as well as Tigga was. Working at a children's hospital was boring most of the time, but they had some fire ass drama going on at the moment.

"I'm sure you heard me the first time, but I don't mind repeating myself. Amari is my baby, so you and your people can leave," Rich repeated confidently.

Red, the color of anger and blood, was what Tigga was seeing as soon as the words left Rich's mouth the second time. In one swift motion, he was up on Rich, delivering a blow to his face that knocked him off of his feet. Thankfully, the security guards were quick on their feet, but Tigga was like a raging bull. As soon as Rich hit the floor, he was on him like a magnet. Rich wasn't expecting the attack, but he did have enough sense to try and fight back. For every lick that he threw, Tigga countered with two or three more. Tigga's adrenaline was pumping and Rich's licks seemed to infuriate him more. Security was doing a piss poor job of breaking them up and Rich felt his eye swelling already.

"Tigga, baby, stop! Calm down before you get arrested," Christy pleaded with her son. Tigga usually kept his cool through any situation, but the information that he'd just received was enough to set anyone off.

"Get the fuck up off of me!" Tigga growled, once two more security guards came and pulled him away. They had seen the drama unfold on the security cameras and rushed right up to help their co-workers.

"I can't believe what I'm hearing. Is what he said true Anaya?" Christy asked.

Tigga looked over to Anaya, waiting for an answer that never came. He knew right then and there that what the other man said was true. He had never put his hands on a woman before, but he wanted to knock Anaya's hoe ass out right there in the hospital's hallway.

"Yeah, it's true and we got a paternity test to prove it," Rich spoke up through his swollen mouth.

"Rich, just leave! You've already caused enough trouble!" Donna yelled at him.

Her daughter was indeed guilty, but she wasn't about to stand there and let them make her out to be the bad person. Her granddaughter was laid up in the hospital and nobody seemed to have any compassion. Anaya was crying uncontrollably and she had every right to be. Her secret was out and Tigga was furious. She knew that it was a wrap on the good life that he'd once provided for her. It was back to the trailer park for her and that was definitely something to cry about.

"Nah, he's right. If that's his daughter, let that nigga stay here with that bum bitch. Let's go ma," Tigga huffed as he walked away with Christy hurrying behind him.

"Tigga, wait!" Christy yelled as she ran to catch up with him.

"Not right now ma. Just tell Keller to me in the car," he replied in aggravation.

Christy called Tessa on her phone to let her and Keller know to meet them in the parking lot. She knew that her son was hurting because she was feeling some of his pain. Tigga was too wound up to wait for the elevator, so he jogged down the stairs to the lobby instead.

"What's going on? Is Amari alright?" Tessa asked as she and Keller met Christy at the elevator.

"Tigga wants you to meet him in the car Keller," Christy said as they got on the elevator and rode down.

"Wait, is he leaving?" Tessa asked.

"Yes and so are we. We'll talk about it later," Christy replied as she got off of the elevator and walked away.

"What the hell is going on around here?' Tessa asked to no in particular.

"I don't know, but I'm about to find out. Call me later," Keller said as she hugged Tessa and left.

She spotted Tigga sitting in his truck smoking, with a weird expression on his face. He looked mad and confused, all at the same time.

"Is Amari okay?" Keller asked when she got into the car.

Instead of answering, Tigga just pulled off and headed towards the bridge. He usually didn't smoke whenever Keller or his girls were around, but he was puffing away as he sped towards their destination. Keller wasn't used to seeing that side of him and she really didn't know what to say. She and Tigga hadn't been together very long, so they were still learning each other. By the time Tigga pulled up to his townhouse, Keller had already made up her mind to stay the night at Kia's house. He seemed to need some time to himself and she didn't want to be a burden. He hadn't said anything to her since they left the hospital and she didn't know why.

"What are you doing?" Tigga frowned when he walked into the bedroom and saw Keller packing an overnight bag.

"I think I'm gonna stay the night at Kia's. I can tell that you have a lot on your mind and I don't want to add to it," Kia replied.

"Don't do that Keller. I do have a lot on my mind, but I don't want you to leave. I'm sorry for shutting down on you, but shit is all fucked up," Tigga said as he sat on the bed and pulled her down on his lap.

"You wanna talk about it?" Keller asked as she rubbed his back lovingly.

"Man," Tigga sighed as he rubbed his hand through his waves. "Amari might not be mine."

"What!" Keller gasped, as she looked him in his eye to make sure he wasn't playing.

"Some clown ass nigga named Rich walked up in there claiming to be her daddy."

"Well, how do you know that he's telling the truth?" Keller inquired.

"That nigga ain't lying Keller. He had no reason to. Anaya hoe ass sat there and ain't open her mouth, so I know it's the truth. Dude said they took a blood test and everything. Bitch had me taking care of a baby for almost three years that she knew wasn't mine."

"I still think you should have Amari retested. Just to be on the safe side," Keller suggested.

"Fuck that! I'm getting all three of them tested. I'm not taking no chances with that bitch," Tigga fumed.

"You think your other daughters might be for somebody else too?"

"I don't really know what to think. Up until a few minutes ago, I thought Amari was mine. They all look just like Anaya, so I can't say anything about their features. I wonder what that nigga's real name is. I bet that's who Amari is named after. She gave me some bullshit story about wanting the baby's name to start with an A like hers," Tigga said, shaking his head.

"Who was the man? Have you ever seen him before?" Keller inquired.

"I don't know who that lame ass nigga was. Standing there wearing a dirty ass Polo and some Reebok Classics. Nigga don't even look like he can afford to take care of Amari. That's probably why Anaya lied about her paternity."

"Did you just say Reebok Classics?" Keller said, laughing.

"I was just as surprised as you are. I didn't even think they sold that shit no more." Tigga laughed with her.

He was still heated, but it felt good to laugh. Tigga knew that the situation with Anaya was bound to get ugly, especially since she now knew about him and Keller. Knowing Anaya, she would probably assume that they were messing around long before they ever started. Tigga had never cheated on Anaya before and he didn't owe her an explanation. He had never cheated on any woman that he'd ever been with, but he always seemed to get cheated on. The girlfriend that he had before Anaya claimed that he was too busy, so she sought companionship elsewhere. Keller seemed to be the female version of him and he was hoping that things between the two of them worked out.

"That's Tessa. I'm sure she's calling to talk about what you just told me," Keller said, trying to remove herself from Tigga's lap.

"Man, forget Tessa. Tell her that your man is stressed the fuck out and he need you right now," Tigga replied as he tightened his hold on her.

"Aww boo, I'm sorry about what's happening to you. I wish there was something that I could do to make you feel better," Keller said while pecking his lips.

"Get naked," Tigga instructed. "You already know what you can do to make me feel better."

Keller smirked, but she stood up and stripped out of her clothes, while Tigga sat there licking his lips. She knew that sex wasn't going to solve his problems, but she at least wanted to make her man feel good, if only for a little while.

Chapter 2

"Stop trying to run," Jaden said as he pulled Kia back by her hips and sat her on his face. He grabbed her ass cheeks firmly, as he licked her from front to back like it would be his last time tasting her. Kia's entire body was shaking and she lost count of how many times she came. She was all out of fluids, but Jaden was just getting started.

"Give me a minute to get right Jaden," Kia begged as she weakly tried to move away from him.

Ignoring her pleas, Jaden picked her up and slammed her down onto his huge erection. Kia was dripping wet and tight, making him moan in satisfaction. Jaden had been with plenty of women in his lifetime, but none of them compared to Kia, in or out of the bedroom. He loved everything about her, which was why he had been trying to do right by her lately.

"Open your eyes," Jaden demanded, as he bounced Kia up and down at a steady pace. Kia did as she was told and locked eyes with the only man that she'd ever loved. So many times she'd wanted to give up on their relationship, but he wasn't letting her go that easily.

"Ooh," Kia moaned as she bit down hard on her bottom lip.

"Cum for me," Jaden demanded, as he continued to stroke her insides like the sex expert that he was. As if on cue, Kia felt her walls contracting as she began to do just what he asked her to do. Right as she was trying to come down from her sexual high, he picked her up and placed her back onto his awaiting mouth.

"Oh God! Jaden, wait, please!" Kia screamed. It was of no use.

Jaden devoured her like she was his last meal and he was trying his best to get full. Although he knew that Kia was tapping out, he still flipped her over and onto her stomach. He had thoroughly pleased her and now it was his turn. Jaden was unselfish when it came to sex. He always made sure that Kia was satisfied before thinking about his own pleasure.

"Throw that ass back and stop playing," Jaden said as he smacked her ass cheeks and watched them jiggle. Kia's eyes rolled up to the sky when he spread her cheeks wide and started hitting her spot.

"Fuck! Yes, baby!" Kia yelled as she tried her best to keep up. When Jaden grabbed her neck and started digging deeper, Kia felt like a hose had turned on between her legs. He had her speaking in tongues and even she didn't understand what was coming out of her mouth. Jaden lightly bit her neck and it was over from there. Kia's body started convulsing and she no longer had control of it.

"I got you, baby," Jaden chuckled. Kia's legs got so weak that he had to hold her up, just to keep her from falling to the floor.

"I can't go no more Jaden," Kia said breathlessly.

"Me either. Shit baby, I'm about to come," Jaden said right before he released and collapsed on top of her, never bothering to pull out.

"Thank God I'm on the pill, huh." Kia laughed.

"I wish you wasn't," Jaden said while kissing the back of her neck.

"I bet you do," Kia replied. It was no secret that Jaden wanted more kids, but she just wasn't ready. Their relationship was getting better, but they still had a long way to go. She didn't trust him and that was bad for any union.

"You never told me what you wanted to do today. I want us to go somewhere and celebrate," Jaden said while pulling her closer to him.

After trying for over a year, Kia had finally passed the supervisor's exam at her job. It was hard as hell and she had failed it over five times. Jaden was so happy for her because she had been stressed out waiting for her test results. Kia was happy that she could now work from home or anywhere else remotely and make more money while doing it. She could also make up her own schedule, just as long as she worked the required sixty hours per week. As a supervisor, she would be a salaried employee with up to six weeks of vacation time per year.

"I don't know, but I'll think of something. I need to go to my job and take a picture for my new badge to log into the work computer. Then, I have to get my nails done and drop Jaylynn's bathing suit off to her at Brooklyn's house," she replied.

"I'll take care of Jay. Just go do whatever else you have to do and come back home," Jaden replied.

"You're not cutting hair today?" she asked him.

"It's almost twelve o'clock. I would have been gone if I was. I told you that I want us to do something today."

"Aww baby, that's so sweet of you. Let me get up and get going. I know one of our stops is gonna be the mall. Me and Jay need a few things," Kia said as she hopped up from the bed.

"Why am I not surprised?" Jaden laughed. "Turn on the shower and assume the position. You gon' put in work for what I'm about to spend on your ass."

"Okay baby." Kia giggled as she ran to the bedroom, ready to get her day started.

***

"What is this stupid bitch doing?" Tori mumbled as she fidgeted with the keys that hung from the ignition of her rental car. She had been following Kia around just about all day and her patience was wearing thin. Aside from the nail shop and post office, Kia had gone to her job and she was still there almost an hour later. Tori was trying to catch her somewhere that wasn't too crowded but, since it was a Saturday, that was almost impossible.

"I'm ready to go," her cousin Anna said in aggravation. "We've been following this bitch for hours now."

"I'm not making you stay. You can leave whenever you want to," Tori said as she popped the locks on the doors.

"Bitch, I knew I shouldn't have come with your stalking ass. Just leave the damn man alone. It's obvious that he don't want you. How many numbers do the nigga have to block before you get the picture? You and Anaya are some dumb hoes," Anna said, referring to her sister.

Anaya didn't do right by Tigga when she had him, now she was going crazy because he had moved on with somebody else. When he took her out of the trailer park, she turned her nose up at Anna and everybody else who she had left behind. Now, it seemed as if she would be crawling right back to the same trailer park that she'd tried to shit on so many times before.

"I don't want him either," Tori lied. "I'm just not feeling how he played me. Working for him was my only source of income and he knew that."

Tori was in tears a few nights ago when she ran into Serena at the club. She had been begging Jaden for weeks to give her another change to work for him, but he kept refusing. He lied and told her that work had slowed down, but Serena was telling an entirely different story. According to her, she was overwhelmed and needed someone to help her. She said that Jaden was trying to find somebody to take Tori's place, but he was helping out until then. Tori was pissed and her pockets were drying up. Jaden had been ignoring her for the past few days, but she was about to make him hear her loud and clear. Kia was his weakness. Tori knew that if she laid hands on Kia, she wouldn't have to look for Jaden any longer. He would be coming to find her instead.

"I'm not trying to be out here on no fighting shit Tori. I got kids at home," Anna said, snatching her away from her thoughts.

"Bitch, I already know that you can't fight. You forgot about all the times I had to jump in to save you from getting your ass whooped."

"I had to help your ass a few times too. Let's not forget about when that nigga sent them chicks to beat you down."

"Some help you were. I still walked away with a black eye," Tori snapped.

"You should be happy that you walked away with your life," Anna retorted.

"Here she come," Tori said as she witnessed Kia walking out with her phone glued to her ear. Tori cringed when she saw Kia's smiling face. She hated to think that it was Jaden on the other end, causing her to blush and giggle. She didn't know what it was, but she just couldn't get Jaden out of her system. Although she worked hard and risked her freedom for the money, in Tori's mind, Jaden was providing for her. She'd never had a man to do anything for her before he came along and she didn't want to ever give that up. In her twisted mind, Kia was the only thing standing in the way of them being together. She couldn't accept that Jaden just didn't want her.

"You need to go say what you have to say to her now. I'm getting tired of following her ass all around New Orleans," Anna complained.

Tori looked around the secluded parking lot and thought that her cousin made a good point. It was still daylight, but there wasn't anyone out that she could see. Thinking that the timing was perfect, she started up the car and drove closer to where Kia was parked. Tori pulled up two cars down but decided not to turn her car off. She didn't know how things were going to play out and she would probably have to make a fast getaway.

"I'm not getting out," Anna said while folding her arms across her huge breasts.

"I didn't expect your scary ass to," Tori snapped as she got out of the car. Kia was oblivious to her presence, which made things even better for her. Tori was able to hear more of Kia's conversation the closer she got to her. When she heard her mention her daughter's name, she knew that it was Jaden who was on the other end. When Tori heard her say that she loved him too, something in her snapped and she pulled Kia by her hair, slinging her to the ground. She knew that attacking Kia from behind gave her the upper hand, but Tori didn't give a damn about being fair.

"Ahh!" Kia screamed as she tried to pry the unknown person's hands from her scalp. She didn't get a good look at whoever was attacking her and that only increased her fears. The hospital's parking lot was secluded, so she didn't know what was going to happen to her.

"Bitch! I hate you, bitch!" Tori screamed as she repeatedly hit Kia in the top of her head. Kia immediately recognized the voice as

Tori's and she became livid once she did. Kia was trying to shield her face and untangle her hair, but she couldn't do much of anything with the way that she was positioned. Since she was already on the ground, she decided to wrap her arm around Tori's leg, in hopes of making her fall. Kia felt a little hopeful when Tori went crashing down on the ground right next to her. The grip that Tori had on her hair loosened and she was able to free her hair from her grasp.

"You crazy bitch!" Kia yelled as she rolled over and landed on top of Tori. She had never been much of a fighter, but her adrenaline was working overtime at the moment. She grabbed a handful of Tori's hair and started banging her head against the concrete. Tori was still throwing blows towards her, but Kia was determined to defend herself. The sting of the concrete connecting to the back of her head must have been too much for Tori to bear. After a while, she stopped swinging and tried to grab the back of her battered skull. Kia used that as an opportunity to get a few licks in to her face. She was fucking her up good, until someone pulled her by her hair from behind.

"Get off of my cousin hoe!" a short, chubby woman said as she slung Kia to the side. Her forehead hit the concrete and Kia felt the warm blood trickling down her face soon after. She tried to block out the pain, as she hurriedly stood to her feet before the two women had a chance to come after her again. Kia got into her fighting stance as both women came rushing towards her. Thankfully, they weren't able to get to her again because two of her co-workers came rushing out of the building. She hated that Andre was one of them, but she was happy that he had intervened. He and Kia hadn't said anything to each other ever since Jaden had almost killed him. Andre was walking around with six false teeth in his mouth, as a result of Jaden's erratic behavior.

"You good Kia?" Andre asked, genuinely concerned about her wellbeing. He really liked Kia but being with her just wasn't worth the risk. She had a crazy ass baby daddy and his life was more important than a quick nut. Besides, he couldn't risk the lives of his family just to be with her anyway. Whenever he saw her at work, he passed by her like she was a total stranger.

"Yeah," Kia said as she embarrassingly walked away towards her car.

"Are you sure? You need me to call somebody for you?" Andre offered sincerely.

"No, I'm fine, but thanks," she replied as a steady stream of tears flowed from her eyes. Tori and the other woman had run back to their car and sped away as soon as Andre and her other co-worker appeared. Kia was so happy that she would be working from home from now on. She couldn't stomach the idea of being around her co-workers after what had just happened. It never failed. Every time she and Jaden's relationship seemed to be heading in the right direction, something always happened to halt their progress. She was heated, as she headed to her house to give her dog ass man a piece of her mind.

***

"Baby, I swear, I haven't talked to that crazy ass girl in months. Every time she calls me from a different number, I put it on the block list," Jaden said, trying to convince Kia that he was being truthful with her.

He was furious when Kia came home with dirty clothes and dried up blood on her face. His pressure went through the roof when she told him about Tori and some other bitch jumping her outside of her job.

"I don't wanna hear shit that you have to say. I'm done with you and all of this drama. You still fucking with that bitch and you can't make me believe that you're not," Kia said as she continued to throw clothes into her duffel bag. She had already called Mo and told her that she was coming to stay at her house for a few days. She needed to be away from Jaden or she was bound to go crazy. What was supposed to be a day of celebration turned out to be a day of pure hell.

"Baby, look at me," Jaden said as he turned Kia's face towards him. "I swear on my daughter's life that I'm not messing with her or nobody else. I know I fucked up a lot in the past, but I'm trying to do right by you. I'm not trying to lose you behind my bullshit Kia."

Kia's heart softened a bit, but she'd heard all of that before. Jaden would lie and cheat and be begging and crying for her not to leave him when she found out about it. She was unmoved by his teary eyes and sad face this time. She needed some time away from him and she was determined to get it.

"I'm stressed Jaden. I need some time to myself. I can't keep going through this shit. I feel like I'm going crazy," Kia said as tears slid down her cheeks.

Jaden's heart broke at the sight of her. Kia was his other half and he hated to see her cry. He really was innocent this time though. Tori was crazy as fuck, but he was even crazier. She was out of her mind if she thought that she was getting away with putting her hands on Kia. Her and whatever bitch she was with was going to see him real soon.

"I'm not trying to stress you out baby. I just wanted us to chill and celebrate your promotion. I don't want you to leave though. Just stay here and I'll go spend the night by Brooklyn with Jaylynn," Jaden suggested. He was going to go pay Tori a visit as soon as he left, but Kia didn't need to know that. He was about to pick Quell up and go straight to Tori's sister's house. He wouldn't even be able to sleep until that crazy bitch was handled properly.

Kia wanted to protest, but she knew that the subject was closed when Jaden took her bag and started unpacking her clothes. Once he was done, he walked over to her and pulled her in for a hug. Kia wanted to tell him to stay, but him leaving was best for both of them.

"I love you, baby. I'll call you later," Jaden said as she kissed her lips and walked out of their bedroom. Kia walked to the front of the house and locked up after he left. She set the alarm before dragging her sore body back to her room and into her bed. She was sure that Mo would be looking for her, so she picked up her phone and gave her mother a call.

"Let yourself in Kia; the door is unlocked," Mo said when she answered the phone.

"You can lock up Mo. I'm not coming," Kia replied.

"Y'all made up that fast? It usually takes a few days," Mo said as she walked to the front of her house and locked her door.

"We didn't make up; he left," Kia informed her.

"Of course he did. That way, he can decide how long y'all will stay apart. What happened this time?" Mo inquired.

Kia would never tell Mo about the fight that she had with Tori. Her mother would be out for blood if she did. Instead of reveling the truth, she downplayed the situation, just like she did every other time.

"We got into it just like always. I'm just so sick and tired of going through the same thing with him."

"Nah, you ain't tired. Keller was tired and she showed that by leaving Leo and moving on with her life. You've been going through the same shit with Jaden for years and nothing is going to change. He's not doing anything more than what you allow him to do. That nigga know that you ain't going nowhere and he uses that to his advantage."

"It's not like I've never left him before. Thanks to Jaylynn, he always finds me," Kia clarified.

"Don't try to blame it on Jaylynn. You wanna be found, which is why you do a poor ass job of hiding. You don't even realize that you have the upper hand. With the way that Jaden loves you, you can make his ass jump through hoops. But only you'll know when you've really had enough. I can't make that decision for you. Call me later," Mo said before she hung up the phone.

Mo had, once again, given Kia a lot to think about. Everything that she said was right. Jaden did what he did because she allowed him to. She called the shots most of the time and he did whatever she wanted him to do. The only time Jaden ever took control of any situation was when he was upset with her, just like he was when he found out about her and Andre. If Kia were to be honest with herself, she would admit that she was scared to start over. She had never really dated anyone because Jaden was all that she knew. She was a sophomore in high school when they met and they grew into adulthood together. She was comfortable and that was a huge problem. Kia knew that things in her life had to change and soon, because she was tired of going through the motions. Honestly, she was ready to pack up and walk away from it all, including Jaden.

Chapter 3

Tigga ran his hand across his face and sighed when he pulled up to his grandparents' house. He knew that his father was there because he saw the raggedy, taped up bike that Terrell often used as his form of transportation. Tigga had enough to deal with already and he wasn't in the mood for Terrell's bullshit. He was only there because his grandfather, Bo, wanted to talk to him. Over a week had passed since the situation with Amari occurred and Anaya was being a bitch already. Tigga asked her for a paternity test on the girls and she went crazy. She swore that Keller was getting in his head, but Keller didn't have anything to do with his decision.

"Hey my baby. How you feeling?" Tigga's grandmother, Mary, asked him as she stood up from the kitchen table to greet him.

She had the house smelling good as always, with whatever meal she whipped up for the day. Mary was old school and she made sure that her husband had a hot meal on the table every single day. She had always been a house wife, so that was her only job and she did it well.

"I'm good," Tigga said, giving his grandma a hug. "Where is Bo?"

"He's in the den waiting on you. I'm so sorry about everything that happened Tyler. You know we're here for you if you need us," Mary said, rubbing her grandson's back lovingly. She loved her great-granddaughters to death and she was heartbroken to find out that one of them might not be his. She still wasn't convinced and she wouldn't be until a blood test told her different.

"I know grandma," Tigga replied, not really wanting to talk in front of his father.

"Well, hello to you too son," Terrell said with a mouth full of food.

Tigga looked at him and frowned, before he walked off in search of his grandfather.

"I'll fix you a plate and bring it to you, baby!" Mary yelled after him.

"Y'all need to stop catering to that nigga. He's a grown ass man and y'all still treat him like a baby," Terrell snapped angrily.

"Hush up Terrell. He's not in a good mood right now," Mary said, defending him.

"Apparently, he's never in a good mood. Nigga walk by me like he didn't come out of my nut sack," Terrell fumed.

"That's your own fault. You don't know how bad you hurt your family when you chose drugs over them. He needed his father, but you weren't there. We had to step in and do your job so, in a sense, he is our baby," Mary replied.

"You don't think I know how bad I fucked up. I have to live with that shit every day, but I don't need to keep being reminded of it. That nigga act like he's better than me. Bo gave him that company just to hurt me, but it's all good," Terrell replied.

"You couldn't run anything being addicted to drugs. Since he took over, Tyler is making more money for the company than you or Bo ever made combined. He's qualified and he proved that a long time ago."

"You would say that. Tigga don't do no wrong in y'all eyes. Tessa messed up one time and she got sent away for years," Terrell acknowledged.

"That was for her own safety and she didn't have a problem with it. You sound like you're jealous of your own son," Mary argued.

"Fuck that lil nigga," Terrell spat angrily.

"It's time for you to go. You will not sit here and disrespect my home," Mary said as she grabbed his empty plate and sat it in the sink.

"You don't care about me disrespecting your house. You just don't want me saying nothing about your perfect grandson. That nigga is living my life, but wanna act like he's better than me. Nigga won't even let me meet my grandkids," Terrell said, right as he walked out the door and slammed it behind him.

Mary just shook her head and continued to fix Tigga something to eat. Once his plate was piled high with a home cooked meal, she grabbed a bottle of water from the fridge and headed down the hall to the den.

"So, when are we going to see Keller again? She's such a sweetheart," Mary said while handing Tigga his plate.

"I don't know. Maybe we can come over for dinner again soon," he replied, right before his grandmother left.

Mary was a sweet old lady and there wasn't a person that she met and didn't like. She was just about the only one in Tigga's small family who genuinely liked Anaya. She took a liking to Keller as soon as they met, but Tigga wasn't surprised by that.

"Your son gon' make me knock his crack head ass out," Tigga vented to his grandpa, once his grandmother had left the room.

"Fuck Terrell! He made his choice on what was more important to him. He chose crack over his family, so he has to live with that," Bo replied angrily.

Bo was a laid back seventy-year-old man who didn't look a day over sixty. He was still vibrant and that's what Tigga loved the most. He could be himself and speak freely around his grandfather, but he knew to watch his mouth whenever Mary was in the room.

"I started to turn around when I saw his bike out there," Tigga said in between bites of food.

"You already know that him being here ain't on me. I washed my hands with his ass a long time ago. That's your grandma with that soft heart, always wanting to feed him and shit. If his ass can afford crack, then he should be able to afford a hot meal. Only child or not, I don't feel sorry for that nigga. But it makes her happy, so I let her have that," Bo replied.

"I guess that's a mother's love." Tigga shrugged.

"But, enough about that. I got Mark to draw up that subpoena for you. He should be sending it out any day now," Bo said, referring to his lawyer.

"Good, I'm tired of playing games with her stupid ass. If she don't agree to share custody, then I'm taking her ass straight to court. She make me think she got something else to hide," Tigga replied.

"Ain't no telling, but what about the apartment? You letting her stay there or what?" Bo questioned.

"I really don't have a choice. I'm not trying to do my kids dirty like that. If it wasn't for them, her ass would be right back in that trailer park."

"Don't you be paying no rent on a place that another man gon' be laying up in," his grandpa warned him.

"You know I'm far from being stupid. My name ain't on the lease no more, so she can move whoever she want up in there. She better make sure she can afford to keep the bills paid though," Tigga replied.

"I told you that I didn't like her from the first day you introduced her to us. Her ass looked sneaky and she tried too hard to be liked. Your grandma likes everybody, so I can't go by her intuition."

"What about Keller?" Tigga asked, just to see what his grandfather had to say about her. Bo never had a kind word to say about anyone that he and Tessa introduced him too, so he was bracing himself for the negative comments.

"What about her?" Bo questioned.

"How do you feel about her?" he asked.

"She got my vote," Bo said as he stood to his feet.

"Whaaaat!" Tigga sang dramatically. "You giving somebody the green light?"

"It's all in the eyes son," Bo said, pointing to his own pupils.

"What about her eyes?" Tigga asked.

"They're sincere. You know what they say. The eyes are the window to the soul," Bo said, leaving Tigga with something to think about.

Chapter 4

"I knew that shit was gonna blow up in your face. No need to sit here and cry about it now," Donna said to Anaya as she wiped tears from her eyes.

"I don't need to hear a speech right now, okay? I got enough on my plate as it is," Anaya snapped.

"Don't get mad with me. You need to fault the nigga that ratted you out. You should have known that wasn't gon' last forever," Donna said as she grabbed her purse and walked out of her house.

Anaya walked out right behind her and took a seat on the wooden steps. It was a little after noon, but she was off from work for the entire weekend. Her intentions were to take her girls to the park for a while, but that plan got derailed once she was served with a subpoena. Not only was Tigga requesting a paternity test for Amari, he wanted one for all three of the girls. Anaya was heated, but she knew that somebody had to be in Tigga's ear to make him go that route. More than likely, it was Tessa or Keller, but she wasn't sure. Maybe his grandfather was the one who suggested it, since he didn't like her very much. Anaya just kept staring at the paper in her hands, as if the wording would magically disappear, but that was just wishful thinking.

"Can we go by our daddy today?" Anaya's daughter, Tia, asked for the hundredth time in the past week.

"No! Stop asking me the same damn question. Get your sisters, and y'all come outside and play for a while," Anaya replied in aggravation.

Almost two weeks had passed since Tigga found out about Amari and she hadn't let the girls go by him since then. She was embarrassed about how everything went down, and she wasn't ready to face Tigga just yet. Plus, the idea of him being with Keller wasn't sitting too well with her either. Thoughts of them sneaking around behind her back had her heated.

"What brings you around this way so early in the day?" Erica asked her when she walked up on her. She was outside watching her kids play when she spotted Anaya walk out of Donna's house. Anaya rarely came around during the day and she never stayed long whenever she did.

"I needed to talk to my mama about something," Anaya replied as she watched her girls ride up and down the sidewalk on their scooters. They were supposed to be riding them at the park, but she was no longer in the mood to do anything.

"Did you talk to Rich yet?" Erica asked.

"No and I don't want to," Anaya snapped.

"What are you mad at him for? That's not his fault."

"I don't know why the hell it's not. He had no business coming to that hospital with that bullshit. All of this could have been avoided."

"You can't be serious. He came there to see about his daughter. You need to stop thinking about yourself for once!" Erica yelled.

"I wasn't thinking about myself; I was thinking about my kids. Rich can't do a damn thing for us, so he should have kept his mouth shut."

"You knew he couldn't do nothing for you when you laid down with him. That's not fair Anaya. My cousin loves you and you shit on him every chance you get. His love for you is the only reason that he agreed to go along with your lie about Amari in the first place."

"No, he agreed because he got locked up two days after finding out that she was his. My baby wasn't even a week old and his ass was back in jail. There was no way in hell that I was gonna jeopardize my relationship for him and he couldn't even keep his freedom," Anaya replied.

Right before Anaya got pregnant with Amari, she noticed that Tigga was pulling away from her. He was barely at home and he ignored her most of the time when he was. She tried her best to be faithful to him, but his lack of interest drove her right into Rich's open arms. At the time, Anaya and Tigga were still sexually active, but she was also having sex with Rich. When she found out that she was pregnant with Amari, she automatically named Tigga as the father. Rich was pissed, but he couldn't do anything without a paternity test.

The day that Anaya and Amari were scheduled to leave the hospital, Rich paid to have a lab tech perform the test on all three of them. He threatened to do just that all while Anaya was pregnant. She just brushed it off because she didn't think that Rich would be able to afford the test. She was shocked when they got the results back naming him as the father. Rich was ecstatic, but his happiness was short lived. Two days after he found out that Amari was his, he got locked up and ended up spending a year in jail. That was when Anaya came up with the bright idea of continuing to let Tigga think that he was Amari's father. She convinced Rich that it would be better for all of them, especially since he wasn't in a position to do anything for his daughter.

Against his better judgment, Rich went along with Anaya's plan, but he'd been regretting it since day one. The only thing that made him feel somewhat better was the fact that he got to see his daughter regularly. His cousin Erica was Amari's Godmother, so she made sure that she had his daughter up there to visit him as often as she could. It also helped that he got to see her when he got out because Erica had her a lot then too. Anaya often sent him money and pictures while he was locked up, but she never came to see him. Amari didn't know Rich as her father and he hated that most of all. Anaya always promised Rich that they would come clean and tell Tigga the truth, but that was a bunch of bullshit. Had he not gone to the hospital and told the truth himself, Tigga would have still been in the dark.

"All of that is irrelevant right now," Erica said after a long pause. "He deserves to be in Amari's life. How do you think that made him feel watching another man bond with his daughter? It's not always about money Anaya. His presence in her life is more important."

"Yeah, well his presence ain't keeping no clothes on her back or food on the table. You're a mother too, Erica. You know how much it cost to raise kids. I know it's not all about money, but let's keep it real; the bills don't get paid without it," Anaya answered, right as Rich pulled up in a raggedy car that sounded like a truck.

"You're right Anaya. You and Rich both have some valid points, but y'all need to sit down and talk it out. I know that's he's been trying to call you, but you've been avoiding him. The cat is out of the bag now. There's no need to be secretive anymore. If y'all are together or not, y'all still have to have a mutual understanding about Amari. Just learn to co-parent."

"I guess," Anaya sighed. "Now, that bastard Tigga is asking for blood test for all three of my kids."

"I know you're lying!" Erica yelled dramatically.

"Nope," Anaya said as she showed her the subpoena. "But I know that's probably his new bitch in his ear with that shit."

"What new bitch?" Erica questioned.

"That nigga showed up at the hospital with his new bitch. The same bitch that came with us to Florida that last time," Anaya answered.

"His sister's friend?" Erica yelled.

"That's the one," Anaya replied as she watched Rich get out of the car and walk into his cousin's trailer. They made eye contact, but she quickly turned her head the other way.

"You should have beat the brakes off of her ass in that hospital," Erica fumed.

"That nigga was acting like her bodyguard, but we gon' see each other again. I'm fucking her up on sight," Anaya swore as she pounded her fist into her open palm.

"I don't blame you," Erica said, right as her phone started ringing. "I gotta go, that's bae."

"You and Tori with these secret men are getting on my nerves!" Anaya yelled to her departing back. She really wanted to go talk to Rich, but she wasn't in the mood at the moment. She had too much on her mind and the upcoming paternity test was right there at the forefront. When her phone rang, displaying Rich's number, she knew that the time for them to talk had come. There was no need to keep prolonging it, so she answered the phone and told him to come outside. Maybe it was time for them to put aside their differences and try to make things between them work. It wasn't like Tigga wanted to be with her, so Rich was the next best thing.

Chapter 5

"I know David said that his wife was sick, but I though Dominic was rolling with us," Tigga said as he sipped from his second drink of the night. He was out at The Penthouse Gentlemen's Club near Bourbon St. with Jaden and two of his brothers. Jaden's other three brothers were cool, but none of them were anything like him. They seemed more laid back, while Jaden was more of a live wire.

"Scary ass nigga bailed on me when he found out that we were meeting at a strip club. I swear, I think Brooklyn got the dick instead of him," Jaden replied as he kept his eyes fixated on the dancer who was performing.

"You talking that shit, but I bet Kia don't know where your ass at," Tigga shot.

"Nigga, I'm far from being stupid. She's already pissed with me."

"For what now?" his brother, Brian, asked him.

"That crazy bitch that use to work for me been on one lately. Hoe mad because I don't deal with her ass no more. She rolled up on Kia at her job and they got into a little scuffle. The bitch is ducking me now, but she can't hide forever. I won't be able to rest easy until I catch up with her nutty ass," Jaden swore.

"Keller told me how crazy she is," Tigga said, shaking his head.

"That bitch is just playing crazy, but I'm certified," Jaden replied. "But, what's up with my sister-in-law? Is that nigga Leo still on that stalker shit?"

"Yeah, his crazy ass still be blowing her up. He can't seem to let go either," Tigga answered.

"That nigga ain't gon' never let go. Keller was probably the best thing that he ever had. I'm telling you, bruh, you gon have to body that nigga sooner or later. He don't have no boundaries. You know I'm down for whatever. Just let me know what it is," Jaden noted.

"Fuck that dude," Tigga said, waving him off.

"Think it's a game if you want to. Love makes people do some stupid shit. That psycho bitch that I dealt with use to follow Kia all around New Orleans, until I got my cousin and her girls to beat her ass. Now, it looks like she's back on that crazy shit again."

"Kia gon' leave your stupid ass. Keep playing with her if you want to," Jaden's brother, Caleb, chimed in.

"Kia ain't going nowhere," Jaden said, waving him off.

"Everybody got a breaking point bruh. That girl gon' get tired of you cheating and doing stupid shit," Caleb replied.

"I ain't doing shit though. Ain't no side bitches or none of that no more. I been spending all of my free time with my family," Jaden replied.

"That's what's up. Me and Keller been hanging tough, but I miss the fuck out of my kids. I ain't never go this long without seeing them. I had to get my lawyer to send Anaya a letter to scare her ass," Tigga replied.

"What happened?" Jaden inquired.

"Her stupid ass agreed to my terms. Starting next week, I'll have them every other weekend and twice during the week when it's not my weekend," Tigga replied.

"You better than me, my nigga. I would have snapped that bitch neck and paid for her funeral. Got you taking care of a baby for damn near three years that ain't even yours," Jaden said as he shook his head.

"I ain't trying to do shit to her hoe ass. Leaving her alone is killing her more than anything. She's really going crazy since she found out that I'm with Keller."

"Y'all took the blood test yet?" Jaden asked.

"Yep, we have to go Monday to get the results," Tigga replied.

"Boy, that'll be some shit if none of them pretty lil girls are yours," Jaden chuckled.

"Nigga, that ain't funny. I'll murder that bitch on sight if that happens. Honestly, I know that the other two are mine. The whole situation with baby number three was in question from day one. We were barely fucking and she swore that she was on birth control. The minute I said I was moving out, she dropped the pregnancy bomb on me," Tigga replied.

"A red flag should have went up right then," Brian butted in.

"You right, but I ignored a lot of stuff for the sake of my kids. I regret that shit now though," Tigga said, shaking his head.

"That's why I'm good with just my one. The only babies I have will be coming from Kia," Jaden swore.

"Nigga, you keep fucking around and you gon' have a whole army out here," Caleb said.

"I keep telling you that I'm chillin'. The only reason I came here tonight is to handle some business," Jaden replied.

"Nigga, what business you got to handle in a strip club?" Brian asked.

"Shaq hooked me up with another runner. Bitch looking to make some extra money and shit for college. I hope she work out better than other one did," Jaden replied, referring to Tori.

"She's a dancer?" Caleb asked.

"Yeah, bitch name Sapphire or Satin. Shit, I don't know; I'm just trying to see what's up with her ass." Jaden shrugged.

He'd gone to see his uncle Shaq a few days ago and got the news that he'd been waiting for. One of the dudes that Shaq was locked up with had a niece who was looking to make some extra cash and help Jaden out. She was a college student who stripped a few nights a week to help pay her tuition. She didn't like working in the club and the money that Jaden was offering would be enough to help her quit. Since Jaden wasn't dealing with Tori anymore, Serena had been putting in mad work all by herself. The extra money was good, but she had been complaining to him about needing more help.

"So, you're telling me that you're here to see a stripper, but it's all about business?" Brian asked, giving his brother the side eye.

"That's exactly what I'm telling you. Man, I'm good on other broads. Within the next six months, Kia gon' have the house and the ring that I've been promising her. I know she's getting fed up with my shit. I can't lose my baby behind the stupid stuff that I be doing," Jaden replied sincerely, right as the DJ announced Black Sapphire as the next dancer to hit the stage.

"That must be your girl," Caleb said as he and the rest of the men turned their attention to the stage.

"Damn," Brian mumbled when a short, dark skinned woman walked on stage dressed in a cat woman costume. They all watched in amazement, as she dropped down low to the floor and started popping and twerking. Jaden's mouth hung open when he watched her go all the way up on the pole and slide down into a split. By then, she was only wearing a thong and metallic gold star pasties to cover her nipples.

"And you want us to believe that everything gon' be all business with y'all?" Caleb asked, as he adjusted the erection that was growing in his pants.

"Man," Jaden drawled as he downed the rest of the Patron that was in his glass. "Hittin' it one time ain't gon' hurt nothing."

"I knew it!" Brian said as he and Caleb fell over with laughter.

"Nigga, you wild. You better chill out before sis be on the first thing smoking on your ass," Tigga warned.

"Man, Kia ain't going nowhere," Jaden said as he got up and walked over to the side of the stage where his new employee had just exited.

***

"Get out baby," Tigga said to Keller when they pulled up to the lab to get his test results. They had called him to pick up the results earlier that morning, but he didn't wake up until almost noon. He was up banging Keller for most of the night, so he was tired as hell. Besides, he didn't want to show up at the same time as Anaya and she probably went early that morning. He and Keller were about to go out to eat not too far away, so it was the perfect time for him to get his results.

"I'm good Tigga. I don't want no drama with your baby mama," Keller replied as she sat on the passenger's side of his truck and scrolled through Facebook on her iPhone.

"Girl, come on and get out. Anaya probably came here this morning," he replied before walking around to open the car door for her.

Keller sighed, but she got out of the truck and grabbed his hand that he had extended out to her.

"Are you nervous?" she asked, right as she and Tigga walked into the building.

"Nope, I already know what the results are gonna say. Two out of three ain't bad." Tigga shrugged like it was no big deal.

"Do any of your daughters have your last name?" Keller asked.

"No, they all have Anaya's last name. I wasn't as mature back then as I am now. I didn't even think to give them my last name and Anaya was cool either way," he replied, right as they walked up to the counter.

"Can I help you?" an older white lady asked them with a smile.

"Yeah, I'm here to get test results for Tyler Coleman," Tigga replied.

"Okay, I'll need to see your identification, but you can have a seat and I'll go get them for you," she replied as she walked away.

Tigga and Keller sat down and watched as she pressed in a code to a door and disappeared inside of a room.

"Damn, they got the results in a secret room or some shit," Tigga said.

"They might. People do so many shady things with blood test nowadays. Smile," Keller said as she pulled out her phone and snapped a selfie of the two of them.

"Girl, you take pictures all damn day." Tigga laughed.

"You laughing, but your ass be right there posing in every one. Now, smile again. I didn't like the last one," Keller replied.

"Where you be putting that shit at?"

"Everywhere. I'm making you Instafamous," she replied as she posted the picture.

"You ain't doing nothing but pissing your ex nigga off. I know that nigga be stalking you on social media."

"Fuck Leo! I can't wait to get certified to carry my gun. He might be the first person that I shoot," Keller said, making him laugh.

"Shoot that bitch too," Tigga said as he nodded his head towards the entrance where Anaya had just walked in with her mother. She had a mug on her face when she saw him and Keller sitting there, and she didn't try to hide it.

"I thought you said that she came this morning," Keller whispered.

"I assumed that she did, but fuck that rat."

"Why did you bring her here? This is a private matter," Anaya snapped as soon as she got closer to them.

"Ain't nothing private about you being a hoe. Get the fuck away from my girl. She's allergic to sluts," Tigga snapped without even looking up at her.

"Anaya, shut up and stop making a fool of yourself," Donna whispered harshly.

"And make sure you have both of my daughters ready for me Friday," Tigga said, purposely leaving Amari out of the equation.

Keller wanted to speak up on it, but she decided to wait until after they left. Tigga had every right to be pissed, but Amari was still a child. She didn't deserve to be blackballed behind something that she had no control over.

"I don't want my girls nowhere around your bitch!" Anaya snapped angrily.

"That's gonna be kind of hard, seeing as how we live together." Tigga smirked, making Anaya's heart drop. "And make that your last time calling her out of her name."

Anaya was hoping that him and Keller's little fling wasn't anything serious, but it seemed to be more than what she thought it was. They had to have been messing around for a while. There was no way that they had just hooked up and were living together already. Tigga was calling her a hoe, but he was no better than she was.

"Looks like I wasn't the only one with a secret," Anaya said, right as the lady came out of the room and called Tigga's name.

He and Keller stood up and ignored the angry glares that followed them. Tigga showed his I.D. and signed for his results. He thanked the lady who helped him right before ripping the envelope open in front of Anaya and her mother. He looked over the paperwork, before pushing the papers towards Keller for her to read.

"Seriously Tigga!" Anaya yelled when she saw Keller looking over the papers.

"Like I said, have my two girls ready for me Friday," Tigga spat as he grabbed Keller's hand and headed back to his truck. He already knew what the results would be concerning Amari, but he was happy as hell that the oldest two turned out to be his. He probably would have really lost it if they weren't. That was one less issue that he had to worry about now. With Leo being on stalker mode a lot more lately, he was sure that more problems were on the way.

Chapter 6

"What about this one?" Tessa asked Keller as she stepped outside of the dressing room to model the dress for her.

"That's the one sis. It's perfect. You might have to put some shorts on underneath it though. Just in case the strippers wanna get frisky with you." Keller laughed.

She and Tessa were at the mall getting themselves together for Co-Co's upcoming birthday party. He and his friend, Sweets, were giving what they called an all-male review party. It was nothing more than a fantasy party to Keller, but she still looked forward to going. Sweets was part owner of a club where he did drag and that's where the party was being held.

"Okay, go find me another one. You know how I am about buying the same stuff that I try on," Tessa replied as she walked back into the dressing room.

Keller got up from the bench and went back to the rack where Tessa's dress came from to look for another one. Once she found her size, she turned around and headed back to the dressing room. She didn't get far before someone was pulling on her arm to stop her. Being that Leo had been calling and threatening her like crazy, Keller was ready to turn around and go off. The frown on her face softened into a smile when she saw that it was Ryan who was trying to get her attention instead.

"Boy," Keller said as she held her chest. "You was about to get the business."

"I saw you frowning up and shit. Give me a hug girl," Ryan

said as he opened his arms up for Keller. She was so happy to see her old cosmetology classmate that she hugged him with no hesitation.

"I thought you moved to Baton Rouge with your lil girlfriend and opened up your barber shop," Keller said, once they pulled away. She hadn't seen Ryan in over a year, but they remained cool up until the day he left.

"I did, but I've been back for about a month now. I still have my barber shop in Baton Rouge, but I just opened up another one down here too," Ryan replied.

"You're back for good?" Keller asked.

"Yeah. Me and ole girl called it quits and I came back home. My mama wasn't gon' have it no other way."

"Your mama still got you spoiled huh?" Keller inquired.

"You know how she is. I got it bad both ways. I'm the youngest and the only boy. She had a nigga feeling guilty about living a little over an hour away. If she got a cold, she was trippin' about me being too far from home to see about her." Ryan laughed.

"So, you got two shops now? You doing it big," Keller complimented.

"I'm trying man. I'm getting ready to close on my house in a few weeks too."

"That's so good Ryan. I'm happy for you. You always said that you wanted to open up a few barber shops and you did it."

"What's been up with you? You still with that crazy ass dude who wanted to fight everybody?" he asked, referring to Leo.

Every time Ryan and Keller spoke to each other in Leo's presence, he wanted to confront Ryan on some fighting shit. Keller was always nothing more than a good friend to him, but he didn't have to explain that to her insecure ass man. The nigga was ugly as shit, so Ryan understood why he didn't want Keller to get away.

"Hell no!" Keller spat in disgust. "I got me a good one this time."

"That's what's up." Ryan smiled right as Tessa walked out of the fitting room.

"Did you get the other dress?" Tessa asked Keller.

"Yeah, here it is. Ryan, this is my best friend Tessa. Ryan use to be my boy best friend until he moved away," Keller said, introducing the two of them.

"I'm still your boy best friend," he said after he and Tessa greeted each other.

Keller smirked when she saw how Ryan watched Tessa as she walked away. Tessa was on the thick side, but she had a nice figure. Everything she wore looked good on her and she knew it.

"Hello," Keller sang while waving her hand in Ryan's face. "You forgot all about me standing here."

"Huh? Oh, my bad Keller," Ryan said as he peeked at Tessa once again. She was standing at the counter looking at jewelry and she looked even better from behind.

"Just go talk to her," Keller suggested, since he was clearly interested.

"She got a man?" Ryan asked her.

"Tessa?" Keller called out. "You got a man?"

"Bitch, what? You know I don't have no damn man," Tessa said, looking at her like she was crazy.

"She's single," Keller said, looking at Ryan with a smirk.

"Well, thanks," he replied sarcastically as he walked over to Tessa.

"Meet me in Dillard's. I'm going to look for Tigga's stuff!" Keller yelled over her shoulder as she left the two of them talking. Tigga asked her to grab him a few True Religion graphics tees, so that's what she was on her way to do.

***

"Nigga, let's go!" Leo yelled to his brother as he continued to walk around the store.

"I'm coming man. I just need to look at one more thing," Jamal said as he continued to shop.

"You got five minutes and I'm burning the fuck out. You walking round this bitch like a nigga ain't wanted and shit," Leo argued.

He'd been doing his best to lay low, but he was tired of sitting inside all day. Thanks to his mother getting him locked up not too long ago for assault, his probation officer decided that he wanted to violate him. Leo got a lawyer to try to handle things for him, but that was a waste of time and money. His P.O. wasn't budging on his decision. Leo was supposed to turn himself in two weeks ago to do a six-months sentence, but he never did it. He gave up his apartment and moved in with his brother and sister-in-law instead. His address was the only one that his probation officer had and he knew that would be the first place that he looked. His brother didn't have any furniture, so Leo furnished their house from front to back with everything that he removed from his own home. Everything seemed to be going wrong in Leo's life and he couldn't figure out how to get things back on track. Keller use to be the one bright spot in his life, but even she was done with him. She blocked Leo from calling, but that didn't stop him from doing it anyway. He even followed her from work a few times, but he was never able to catch her alone. Every time she left from the shop, she either went to Mo's house or to the house in Metairie with her new nigga. Leo had followed her to the house on several occasions, but he was never able to get pass the security gate. He was so desperate that he even slept out front in his car one night. That was how he was able to see her with her new man. They must have been in her man's truck and Leo almost missed them. That was, until Keller hopped out of the silver Hummer to check the mailbox. He was heated as he followed them to a restaurant and watched them feed each other breakfast in between kisses.

His anger didn't just come from the fact that Keller had somebody else. He was pissed about the possibility of her being with somebody else while they were still together. It was obvious that their relationship had been going on for a while. They seemed too familiar with each other for it to be new. He didn't know who the other man was, but he was determined to find out. He even had his brother's girlfriend send her a friend request to keep up with her on social media. Damn near every picture that Keller posted was of her and her boo. Leo couldn't help but to feel jealous, especially since Keller's new man seemed to have his shit together. He looked just like the pretty boy type that most girls like her went for. Leo knew that he wasn't the best looking nigga and Keller had definitely upgraded.

"Damn man, I'm still not sure about the shit that I picked out. I hate being rushed," Jamal said, snapping Leo away from his thoughts.

"You should have drove your own car and you wouldn't have to worry about that," Leo replied, right as something, or rather, someone, caught his attention.

Leo had to do a double take when he looked across the room and saw Keller picking up shirts from a rack. He looked around for a few minutes to see if anyone was in the store with her. When it appeared that she was alone, Leo started making his way over to her.

"You ready bruh?" Jamal asked him.

"Nah, take your time," Leo said as he continued his stride.

The area where Keller was standing was right next to the fitting rooms. There were no sales associates around, so that was perfect for him. Leo snuck up behind her and put his hand over her mouth, before dragging her into one of the small rooms.

"Mmm," Keller mumbled as she kicked and tried to claw at his hands.

"Bitch, shut the fuck up!" Leo demanded in a sinister tone.

Keller's eyes grew big from fear when she recognized his voice. She was kicking herself for not paying more attention to her surroundings. Being in a crowded mall didn't mean anything if there was no one around to help her. Tears immediately began to pour from her eyes at the thought of what could possibly happen to her.

"The fuck you crying for?" Leo asked as he stared at her reflection in the mirror in disgust. He still had his hand covering her mouth, so she couldn't answer even if she wanted to. He needed to hear what she had to say, so he slowly moved his hand and turned her around to face him.

"Help! Somebody help me!" Keller screamed like a crazy person. And just like before, Leo used fear to try and control her.

"Scream again and, I swear, I'll snap your fucking neck," he whispered as she wrapped his big hands around her neck.

Keller was paralyzed with fear and she had every right to be. Leo was unpredictable and there was no telling what he would do to her. His touch, that she once craved, now sent chills of fear throughout her entire body. Keller looked up at him and realized that Co-Co had been right all along. Leo was ugly as hell, but her love for him had her blinded for years.

"I won't scream. Just please don't hurt me," Keller begged.

"Don't hurt you?" Leo repeated incredulously. "You mean hurt you like you hurt me? You left me to rot in jail while you were running around with another nigga."

"I wasn't running around with anybody. You made a baby on me and you expected me to forgive that? It was bad enough that you beat me every other week. How much did you expect me to take?" Keller cried.

She didn't care if she lost her life in that fitting room. She was not about to tell Leo what he wanted to hear. He made her life a living hell and he needed to know it. It wasn't all his fault because she was dumb enough to stay with him during it all.

"So, you don't live with some nigga in Metairie?" Leo asked, ignoring everything else that she had just said.

"Yeah, I do," Keller replied honestly.

"You was fucking that nigga while we were still together," Leo said as he tightened his grip on her neck.

"No, I wasn't. I never cheated on you. I didn't get with him until after I found out about your baby. I was done after that and I moved on."

It pained Leo to hear her say that she moved on, but he knew that he drove her to it. He knew that Keller would be hurt once she found out about the baby. What he didn't know was that she would leave him behind it. He just figured that he would be able to sweet talk his way out of it, like he did every other time. Leo removed his hands from her neck and grabbed the sides of Keller's face. He'd been with plenty of women in his lifetime, but none of them compared to her. Keller was beautiful inside and out, and he knew that women like that were hard to come by. He had to get her back and he didn't care what he had to do to make it happen.

"I love you, baby. I never meant to do anything to hurt you, Keller. I know that I have to learn to control my anger and keep my hands to myself. Just give me another chance to get it right. We can get us a new place and start over fresh," Leo pleaded.

Unfortunately, his pleas fell on deaf ears. Keller was done and she meant it. She didn't know if she was quite in love with Tigga just yet, but she knew that she didn't want to be without him. It felt good having a man who actually knew how to treat her. She didn't have to watch what she said or what she did. And, most of all, she didn't have to worry about covering up black eyes and bruises or lying to her friends and family about how she got them. Leo was out of his mind if he thought that she was going back to that.

"Let's go somewhere so we can talk," he suggested when Keller didn't say anything. He knew for sure that she was thinking about his proposal, but that was the furthest thing from the truth.

"No Leo, I don't want to talk. I have to go; Tessa is waiting for me," Keller replied.

"Fuck Tessa! We need to figure this shit out Keller. Just tell me what I have to do to make things right," he begged.

"You can't make this right Leo. I've moved on and I'm happy," Keller replied honestly.

Sadly, her honesty only infuriated him more. Not only was Leo upset, but he was hurt as well. He saw it in her eyes. Keller really didn't want him anymore. They were officially done. He just couldn't see himself walking away peacefully, while Keller lived happily with another man. Leo felt like he was dying inside and he wanted Keller to suffer the same fate.

"So, you choosing another nigga over me?" Leo questioned, as his hands found their way around Keller's neck again. His face was a mixture of anger and hurt, while Keller's expression showed fear.

"I can't breathe," Keller choked out right before Leo squeezed, restricting her oxygen.

"I can't breathe without you either," he replied as he continued to choke her. He looked like the devil himself and Keller just knew that she wasn't going to make it out of the fitting room alive. She regretted not listening to her loved ones all the times that they told her to leave him. Maybe things would have turned out differently if she had. Keller's phone started ringing, but she was in no position to answer it. Her body was getting overheated and it felt like she would pass out at any moment. Her first thought was to pray, so that was exactly what she did. She prayed for God to spare her life and she was hoping that He was listening.

"Keller!" Tessa yelled as she walked around in the men's section with her phone glued to her ear, trying to call her friend. She heard Keller's phone ringing and she tried to go in the direction that the sound was coming from. When Leo heard Tessa calling Keller's name, he snapped out of his trance and released her from his tight hold. Keller's petite body dropped to the floor, as she tried to suck in as much air as her lungs would allow her to.

"Fuck! Baby, I'm so sorry!" Leo yelled in panic when he saw what he had done. He didn't mean to do her like that, but he snapped, just like he always did when she made him mad. He paced the small area for a few seconds before opening the door and rushing out to find his brother.

"What the hell did you do to my friend?" Tessa screamed when she saw Leo hurrying from the same direction that she was heading in. Leo looked like he'd seen a ghost as he bypassed her and rushed towards the exit. He never even bothered with trying to find his brother. He needed to get away from the mall and fast.

"Oh my God, Keller! What the hell happened?" Tessa yelled when she saw Keller sprawled out on the floor holding her bruised neck. She was too distraught to answer, so she just grabbed Tessa and cried into her chest.

"It's okay friend. Let me call my brother," Tessa said as she hugged Keller and dialed Tigga's number. She knew that her brother was going to be pissed and he had every right to be.

Chapter 7

"This is the house right here," Jaden said as he, Tigga, and one of his boys pulled up to Leo's mama's house. They had already gone to the apartment that he and Keller shared, but he had moved. Tigga was heated when Tessa called him from the mall to pick her and Keller up the day before. His anger reached new heights when he saw how distraught Keller was. Her neck was badly bruised and Leo's fingerprints were clearly visible. She told him about what happened and he'd been on a mission to find Leo ever since. Jaden was always down for the cause, so he made it his business to roll with him. Pluck, one of Jaden's young customers, rode with them, ready to put in work.

Pluck was an eighteen-year-old savage who had more heart than most grown men twice his age. He was like a younger version of Jaden, which was why they clicked almost immediately. He tried to get Jaden to put him on to make some extra money, but he was too wild and reckless for that. Jaden let him make a few dollars by riding out of town with Tori once when Serena couldn't do it, but that was as far as it went. Besides, Jaden felt that working with females was a lot less stressful. He didn't have to worry about a nigga being jealous and trying to do him dirty for a few dollars. His only problem was keeping the females that he worked with from catching feelings after they got the dick. He still hadn't had any luck catching up with Tori, but he wasn't going to stop looking for her shady ass either. He and Pluck kicked down her sister Toni's door a few nights ago, but that crazy bitch wasn't there. Toni swore that she hadn't seen her sister in a few days, but Jaden didn't believe her. He had Pluck riding through there a few times a day, just to see if she would show up. They hadn't had any luck yet, but she was bound to turn up eventually. Jaden tried calling her phone, but she never answered for him. She already knew what it was, so she was doing the right thing by hiding out.

"You want me to go see what's up Tigga?" Pluck asked from the back seat of Tigga's Hummer when they parked in front of the house.

"Nah, I'm going see myself," Tigga replied as he grabbed his registered gun from underneath his seat.

"No bruh, all of us are going to see. I don't trust that nigga and none of his people," Jaden said as he and Pluck hopped off the truck and followed behind Tigga.

All three men marched up to the front porch, observing their surroundings as they did. Tigga used his closed fist and banged on the door loud enough for the entire block to hear him.

"Who the hell is it?" a woman yelled from the other side of the closed door.

"Open this bitch up and see," Jaden flippantly replied.

Instead of opening the door, they saw someone move the curtain to peep out of the huge front room window.

"Who do you want?" Leo's mother, Pat, asked the three frowning men who were standing on her front porch. She had the phone in her hands, preparing to the call the police if she had to.

"Where Leo at?" Tigga barked angrily.

"Leo don't live here. Get off of my porch before I call the police," Pat threatened as she showed them her cordless phone.

"Stop with the threats my baby. You already know how it is. We can kick this raggedly ass door down and be long gone before they even answer for you. Nobody ain't trying to do nothing to you," Jaden replied.

"Leo don't live here," Pat repeated nervously. She didn't know what her no good ass son had done, but she was sure that it was bad. The men at her door looked like they were ready for war and she was right in the middle of it.

"Man, I'm not in the mood to be going back and forth with you, miss lady. Just open the door and let me holla at you," Tigga said impatiently. Pat was still unmoving, making them that much more aggravated with her.

"Fuck it. We tried to get you to open up. Now, I'm bout' to kick this raggedy bitch off the hinges," Jaden said as he lifted his foot high in the air.

"Wait!" Pat yelled in horror. "I'll open it."

They waited impatiently as she left from the window and moved over to the door. They heard the locks being undone, until Pat finally cracked the door open.

"Please, don't do anything crazy. My grandbaby is in here sleeping," Pat begged.

"Ma'am, I have kids of my own. I'm not trying to do nothing to you or your grandbaby. I just want to know where Leo is at," Tigga said as the three of them stepped inside.

"I really don't know where he's at. I had to call the police on him the last time he came here for beating up on my daughter and her friend. I heard that he went to jail, but I haven't seen him since," she replied. Tigga stayed in the living room conversing with Pat, as Jaden and Pluck checked the house just to be sure. Pat wanted to protest, but she decided not to make matters worse. Besides, she knew if they really wanted to do something to her, they wouldn't have knocked on her door to begin with.

"Leo is your son?" Tigga asked her.

"Unfortunately," Pat replied in disgust. "How do you know his evil ass?"

"Keller is my girlfriend," Tigga replied.

"So, she finally left his ugly ass alone huh? It's about damn time. What, is he still bothering her or something?" Pat questioned.

"Something like that," Tigga answered, right as Jaden and Pluck walked back to the front of the house.

"That nigga ain't here, but I'm sure she know where he's at," Jaden said, pointing to Pat.

"I swear to you that I don't. I haven't seen that boy in a while and I don't want to see him," Pat replied. Leo was more than likely by her son Jamal or one of her nephews, but she would never tell them that. It was bad enough that they were at her house. She didn't feel comfortable involving anybody else in Leo's mess.

"Let's go," Tigga said as he walked out of the house and back to his truck, with Jaden and Pluck following. He was mad that he couldn't find Leo, but that wasn't going to stop him from trying.

"Now what?" Pluck asked them.

"That nigga can't hide forever. You'll catch up with him eventually," Jaden said.

"I don't even know how the nigga look. Aside from saying that he's ugly, nobody is telling me shit," Tigga complained.

"Keller don't have no pictures of his ass?" Jaden questioned.

"She deleted all of them," Tigga answered.

"Let me ask Kia if she still got pictures of that nigga in her phone. I know we took pictures with him and Keller a few times when we went out together," Jaden said as he dialed Kia's number.

Tigga and Pluck talked to each other, while Jaden talked on the phone with Kia. A few minutes later, Jaden got off of the phone and waited for his messages to come through.

"Here he go," Jaden said as he passed Tigga his phone to look at the four pictures that Kia had just sent to him.

"This is the nigga that was putting his hands on my baby? Fuck boy look just like the crypt keeper," Tigga snapped as his face twisted in anger. Jaden and Pluck fell out laughing, but he was serious as a heart attack. He wasn't the type to call another nigga ugly, but there were no other words to describe Leo.

"Where sis at right now?" Jaden asked, referring to Keller.

"She's with Tessa by my grandma's house. I'm going get her in a minute so we can go get my girls," Tigga replied.

"You going back to the strip club to see Bianca tonight Jaden?" Pluck asked, excitedly referring to the dancer that Jaden had working for him now.

"Ole girl fake as fuck," Tigga chimed in. "All that shit she was talking about her education coming first and being tired of dancing. That was a bunch of bullshit."

"She was talking all that education shit and I had her bent over the trunk of her car in the parking lot the same night." Jaden laughed. "But, she don't need to quit the club. That's where she makes all of her sales at."

"Pills sell fast anywhere you go," Tigga replied

"So, are you going back to the club or what? I'm ready to chill," Pluck said, trying to go see some naked women.

"Nah, you can drop us off to my car by the shop. Me and my young boy are still on the hunt for this bitch who's been hiding from me," Jaden told Tigga, referring to Tori.

"You better be careful bruh. Her crazy ass might try to get you locked up," Tigga warned.

"I'm not doing nothing to that hoe. Pluck got five sisters and they're all ready to put in that work. I just need to find out where she's at and they'll take care of the rest," Jaden replied.

"Damn boy. You got five sisters?" Tigga asked Pluck.

"Yep and six brothers. It's twelve of us, all under twenty-five years old," he replied like it was nothing.

About ten minutes later, Tigga was dropping them off to Jaden's car before heading over to his grandma's house. After going in to speak to his grandparents for a few minutes, he and Keller were on the way to pick up his daughters. He was supposed to get them the week before, but they had some kind of stomach virus. He made sure to visit them every day, but he decided to let them get well before taking them for the weekend.

"What you wanna eat tonight baby?" he asked Keller when they were in route to Anaya's house.

"It doesn't matter to me. Maybe you should let the girls decide," she replied, right as they pulled up to the house.

"I'll be right back," Tigga said as he got out of the car and jogged up the stairs.

Keller laughed when the front door flew open and one of his daughters met him on the porch. She was so excited to see him and he seemed to have felt the same way. Keller waited patiently as he walked into the house to get their belongings. It only took about five minutes before they were all walking back out. Keller was pissed once they pulled away from the house and turned the corner to get on the bridge.

Tigga was puzzled when he got back into the car and saw the frown that covered Keller's face. She was fine just a minute ago, so he didn't know what her problem was.

"What's wrong?" he asked as he looked over at her.

"Turn around and go back," Keller demanded.

"What? Why?" Tigga questioned.

"Go back and get Amari," Keller insisted.

"Hell no Keller! Are you serious right now?" he asked in shock.

"I'm dead ass serious. I really can't believe you right now Tyler."

"What did I do?" he asked, genuinely confused.

When Keller shook her head and folded her arms across her chest, he was really lost. She only did that when she was mad, but he didn't do anything wrong. Tigga didn't want to argue in front of his daughters, so he pulled his truck over in a grocery store parking lot and got out. Keller took off her seatbelt and joined him at the back of his truck.

"What's the problem?" Tigga asked while looking down at her.

"Why did you take them and leave Amari?"

"What you mean? You were there when I got my test results, right?" he quizzed.

"I know she's not yours Tigga, but she's still your daughters' sister. You're really the only father that she's ever known. Do you really think she understands why you picked her sisters up and left her there? She's a baby. Don't take your anger out on her. That's not fair," Keller argued, making him feel guilty.

Amari cried when Anaya told her that she couldn't go with her sisters and he was sure that she didn't understand what was going on. Keller was right. None of what was happening was her fault. She was an innocent child caught up in an adult situation. He wasn't sure if Rich was in her life or not, and he really didn't care. He was all that she knew and he still loved her the same.

"Damn man," Tigga sighed, feeling bad as hell. "Let me call and tell Anaya to get her ready."

"Thank you, baby." Keller smiled, making him smile in return.

He couldn't even lie to himself. If Keller wasn't with him, there was no way that he would have thought about bringing Amari along. Tigga knew that he could be mean at times, but Keller was determined to bring the best out of him while they were together.

Chapter 8

"Ugh! Why are you always so rough?" Bianca complained, as Jaden curved her body over her sofa and pounded into her with no mercy. He was never gentle with her, even after she voiced her dislike of his treatment.

"Shut the fuck up!" Jaden growled as he gripped her cheeks and dug in deeper than before. Bianca wanted to scream for him to stop, but she didn't want to piss him off. For some strange reason, she really liked his crazy ass, even though she couldn't figure out why. Jaden was an outspoken asshole most of the time, but he was always upfront and honest.

"Ooh shit baby, you're hitting my spot!" Bianca screamed through her pain filled pleasure.

"You talk too fucking much. Just be quiet and take the dick," Jaden said as he grabbed a handful of her weave.

Bianca yelled out in pain, since it felt like the stiches were being ripped right from her scalp. When Jaden roughly grabbed her neck and shoved her face down into the pillows, Bianca felt like she was suffocating. He threw one of her legs over the arm of the sofa, putting her in a terribly uncomfortable position. Not to mention, her womanly parts felt like they were on fire because he was being so brutal. His face was void of any emotions and he didn't look like he even wanted to be there.

"Jaden, stop. You're hurting me," Bianca said as tears threatened to spill from her eyes. She tried to endure the pain, but she couldn't take it anymore. Jaden had never been the gentlest lover, but he was almost violent with her that time. It was only their third time having sex, but there was nothing pleasurable about it.

"The fuck you begged me to come over here for then?" he snapped in irritation.

"I just wanted to spend some time with you before I went to work. You were the one who wanted your dick sucked," Bianca spat.

"And that's all I wanted. You were the one who wanted to fuck. Fuck I look like coming here just to chill with you," Jaden said right before pulling the condom off and disappearing into her half bathroom.

Bianca limped to the other bathroom in her bedroom and wet a towel to freshen up. She cringed when she wiped in between her legs and saw faint traces of blood on the towel. Her hair was a mess and a few of her tracks were hanging by a thread. After cleaning herself up and putting on a robe, Bianca made it back to her living room, right as Jaden was coming out of the bathroom.

"I need more pills. A few people are coming by tonight to get some," Bianca said while taking a seat in her recliner.

"You sold everything?" Jaden questioned.

"Yeah, let me get your money," she said as she stood up and walked back to her bedroom. Jaden walked out of the house and to his car to get her more products. When he came back inside, Bianca was sitting on her sofa sorting out a pile of bills.

"I hope you ain't dumb enough to be doing that shit out in the open," Jaden said as he bagged up some pills for her to take to the club.

"I'm not crazy Jaden. They know to meet me in the back by the private rooms. Are you coming through tonight?" she asked him.

"Nope, I'm spending the day with my girl," Jaden said, making her frown.

"What about me?" Bianca asked.

"What about you? If you trying to catch feelings, we can end this shit right now. I just went through that with the last bitch I had working for me. You know I got a girl, so don't even go there," Jaden warned.

"I told you that sex complicates things for me. That's why I didn't want to go there with you. We should have just kept this shit professional and not crossed that line."

"You're right, point taken. From now on, it's all about the money and nothing else," Jaden said, like the decision was simple.

"So, we're done just like that?" Bianca asked with a snap of her fingers.

"We never really started. It was just sex. Don't make the shit out to be more than what it was. You knew what it was from day one. I hate emotional ass females. Finish counting up the money, so I can get the fuck on," Jaden frowned.

Bianca sorted through the money and counted it out to Jaden. Once he gave her what he owed her, he tossed her some more pills and stood to his feet, preparing to leave. Bianca didn't want him to leave upset, so she stood in front of the door, blocking his path.

"I apologize Jaden. I know I can be too emotional at times, but I promise to keep my feelings in check from now on," Bianca promised.

"You're good Bianca. I shouldn't have went there with you in the first place. I was doing good being faithful to my girl and I need to get myself back on track." He shrugged.

"When am I gonna see you again?" she asked, sounding almost desperate.

"Hit me up when you run out and I'll drop off some more."

"That's not what I meant. When am I gonna see both of you again?" she asked while grabbing at his crotch.

"You won't, that's a done deal," Jaden said, slapping her hand away.

"Don't be like that Jaden. I promise I won't get emotional anymore," Bianca said as she dropped down to her knees in front of him.

Jaden didn't move, as she unfastened his belt and pulled his erection from his Ralph Lauren boxers. Bianca licked her lips seductively, right before she put him into her mouth and went to work. Jaden's head fell back against the door, while his hands instinctively grabbed the back of Bianca's head. Her scalp was still tender, but she didn't want to complain. She got excited when she heard the moans of pleasure coming from Jaden and that only made her want to work harder. She started really getting into what she was doing, right as Jaden's phone started ringing. Usually, he would let his calls go to voicemail, but she knew, without a doubt, that he was about to answer. Whenever the song, Wifey by Next blared from his phone, everything shut down.

"Move!" Jaden yelled as he pushed her head away. "Don't say nothing."

"Um, this is my house you know," Bianca said from her position on the floor.

"Open your mouth and my fist is going in it," Jaden threatened with an angry glare.

"Whatever," Bianca mumbled to herself.

"What's up baby?" Jaden asked as his entire demeanor changed. Bianca hated when his girlfriend called because he was a completely different person. She always eavesdropped on his conversations, so she knew what both of them were saying.

"Make sure you're home no later than two o'clock Jaden. We're going all the way to Baton Rouge and you know how that traffic is. I don't want to hear any excuses!" Kia yelled.

"I know baby, I won't be late," Jaden promised as he pulled his boxers and pants back up.

Bianca wasn't done, so she tried to pull them back down. When Jaden grabbed a handful of her hair and scowled at her, she held her hands up in surrender and backed away from him. She stood there staring at him with her arms folded across her chest, like he owed her something. Leaving her alone was for the best and Jaden knew exactly what he had to do.

"Okay, I'm going to drop Jay off to your mama. I'll see you when you get home," Kia said.

"I'm on my way now," Jaden said before they disconnected.

"Was it really that serious Jaden?" Bianca asked while massaging her sensitive scalp.

"Hit me up when you run out of pills. Don't call me for shit else, if you don't want to get your feelings hurt," Jaden said as he adjusted his clothes and walked out of her front door.

He was officially done. Not just with Bianca but with any other female if it wasn't Kia. He was being stupid and he knew it. He didn't even have a reason to cheat, except for the fact that he knew he could. It also didn't help that he fucked around and cheated with some of the craziest bitches that he'd ever come across. It was bad enough that Tori was a nut case; he didn't need Bianca on some crazy shit too. The only way for him to assure that nothing like that happened was for him to keep his dick in his pants and be faithful.

***

"Wait a damn minute. I wasn't ready," Co-Co screeched as the instructor tried to show him the proper shooting techniques.

He decided to go with Keller and Kia to Baton Rouge to get certified to carry a gun. Both women had on headphones to drown out the noise, but he refused to wear his.

"Co-Co, shut your fruity ass up. Put the damn things on your ears if you gon' scream every time a gun go off," Jaden fussed.

"I'm not putting that shit on my ears and mess my hair up," Co-Co argued.

"Which one of y'all invited this nigga?" Jaden asked, looking at Keller and Kia.

"I did, so leave my boo alone," Keller replied.

"Your boo?" Tigga questioned with raised brows.

"Tigga, please," Co-Co blurted out. "Keller is fine and all, but there ain't a bitch that's been born that can turn me straight."

"I want a pink gun with the matching bag," Kia said, looking over at Jaden.

"Whatever you want baby," he replied while smiling down at her.

"When do we get out certification papers?" Co-Co questioned the instructor.

"Your scary ass might not even get one. You didn't even hit none of the targets," Jaden replied before the instructor had a chance to.

"You go stand out there. I bet I can shoot your ass," Co-Co said, making Tigga and the other man laugh.

"Don't mind them sir. This is how they show love to one another. They do this every day at work," Keller said, waving them off.

"To answer your question, we can do your fingerprints and notarize your paperwork here. You'll get your papers in the mail within ten to fifteen days, maybe sooner. You don't really need a permit to carry in Louisiana, but it's good to have if you plan to conceal a weapon," he advised.

"You ain't gon' shoot nobody, but Dwight anyway." Jaden laughed.

"Why are you even here? The last time I checked, convicted felons couldn't even own a gun," Co-Co snapped.

"Shit, that ain't never stop me before," Jaden said, giving Tigga dap.

Tigga had never gone to jail, so he didn't have those kinds of problems. It was never a problem for Jaden either. He had an arsenal of weapons and they were all clean. After taking a few more practice shots, Kia, Keller, and Co-Co did their paperwork and purchased their weapons. Keller had recently gotten an eighteen-month long restraining order on Leo, but she felt better protected knowing that she would have a gun with her. She was really afraid of guns, but Tigga stressed to her how important it was for her to carry one. After what happened to her in the mall, he didn't have to tell her twice. She knew that she couldn't bring a weapon in certain places, but she would make sure that she could get to it when and if she ever needed it.

Chapter 9

"Don't forget Keller. We're going out to eat and have a few drinks. That's the story that you and Tessa need to stick with," Kia whispered to her sister over the phone.

"I got you, Kia. You don't have to keep drilling it in," Keller replied.

"Okay, I'm going by Mo to get dressed. I'll call you when I'm done," Kia said before she hung up the phone.

Jaden would have a fit if he knew that she was going to Co-Co and Sweets' male review party, which was why she didn't bother with telling him. He was already calling it a freak party and Kia was about to be in the building right with the other freaks. Tigga probably wouldn't have tripped about Keller going, but she had to lie to him too. Jaden knew that if Keller was going, then Kia would be there too.

"Is the food done?" Jaden asked as he walked into the kitchen wearing his pajamas that he had just changed into. He and Jaylynn had a pile of junk food set up in the front room and Kia was frying them some fish and shrimp.

"Almost," Kia replied. "Did Jay take her bath?"

"Yeah, she did. I hope she wants to watch one of the movies that I got for her. I'm tired of watching Matilda. I swear, I hate that lil girl and she ain't never did shit to me," Jaden fussed, making Kia laugh.

He complained about the same thing all the time, but he did whatever Jaylynn wanted him to do. Jaden had been staying close to home and it felt good spending time with his family. True to his word, he had given up dealing with other females and it had been almost a month since his last encounter with Bianca. Once he left her house that last time, he didn't see her again unless he was making a drop off or pick up at the club. He was serious about remaining faithful to Kia and he was ready to lock her down and put a ring on it. Brooklyn had been helping him look for the perfect diamond to grace Kia's fingers and he was ready to buy it as soon as he found it. He was sorry that it took him so long to get his mind right, but it was better late than never.

"Y'all should have everything that y'all need now," Kia said as she eyed all the food that she had spread out on the table for Jaden and their daughter.

"Yeah, we're straight. You look good baby," Jaden complimented as he looked Kia over from head to toe. She wore a pair of ripped skinny jeans with a black and silver fringed shirt and wedges to match. Her hair was wand curled and cascaded down her back like running water.

"Thanks boo." Kia smiled.

"Let me walk you out," Jaden said, getting up from the sofa. "Call me when you're on your way back, so I can meet you outside."

"I will," Kia promised.

"I love you," Jaden said before kissing her lips.

"Love you too," Kia said, right before she pulled off and headed to Mo's house. Jaden watched her until she was out of sight before he went back inside to join in his daughter in the living room.

"Alright baby girl, what are we watching?" he asked Jaylynn, even though he was dreading the answer.

"Um," she said as she looked up to the sky like she was thinking about it. Jaden hoped that she was, but he should have known better. "How about Matilda?"

"Matilda it is," he said, grabbing the remote to find the recording. He had spent almost one hundred dollars on movies, hoping that she would like at least one of them. She only opened one of the movies and complained about it the entire time that it was on.

"You want me to fix you some food daddy?" Jaylynn offered.

"Yeah, hook me up," Jaden replied.

He and Jaylynn pigged out for a while and watched movies. Jaden was happy as hell when he put on the movie Child's Play and Jaylynn seemed to be enjoying it. He promised her that he was going to buy her all parts of the movie the following day and that was a promise that he was going to keep. Having her watch a movie about a killer doll wasn't very healthy for a girl her age, but anything was better than Matilda.

"Your phone is ringing daddy," Jaylynn yelled when Jaden was in the bathroom. It had been over four hours since Kia left and they were about to watch their third movie.

"I'm coming baby," Jaden said, right as he washed and dried his hands. The phone had already stopped ringing, so he called Dominic right back to see what he wanted.

"What's up with you, nigga?" Dominic said as soon as he answered the phone.

"Ain't shit. I'm chilling with Jaylynn while Kia have her a girls' night out," Jaden replied.

"I'm in here with my three lil ones too. Kia must have went to that bullshit ass party that Co-Co and Sweets gave, huh?" Dominic asked.

"Nah, she went out for drinks with Keller and Tessa," Jaden replied.

"She went out for drinks alright. She right there with my wife and Candace at Co-Co and Sweets' party. Nigga, you better start checking social media. They partying hard like a muthafucker." Dominic laughed.

"Man, you know I don't do that online shit, but I know Kia ain't at that damn freak party," Jaden said angrily.

"Hold on one second," Dominic told him. Jaden heard him shuffling around, right before he came back to the line. "Check your phone."

He didn't have to tell Jaden twice. He removed the phone from his ear and scrolled through the pictures that Dominic had just sent him. He was heated when his gaze fell upon Kia. She had on a totally different outfit than the one she left in and her face was covered in makeup. Keller, Tessa, and Brooklyn were right there with her while half-naked men posed behind them in the background.

"I'm fucking her up on sight," Jaden fumed as Dominic fell out laughing on the other end of the phone.

"You ain't gon' do shit, but try to lock her inside for a few days. Let that damn girl make it. She works hard and takes care of your daughter. She deserve a break sometimes," Dominic reasoned.

"Man, fuck what you saying. You might be alright with other niggas slanging dick in Brooklyn's face, but that shit ain't gon' fly with me," Jaden replied.

"Nigga, I'm not trippin' over no bullshit like that. Brooklyn sleeps next to me every night, so another man is never a threat. Your ass cheat so much that it kills you to think that Kia is doing the same thing," Dominic said, calling him out.

"So, what you saying? You think Kia fucking around on me?" Jaden inquired.

"Bye bruh. Go spend time with Jay and leave Kia alone," Dominic said right before he hung up. Jaden heard what his brother-in-law had said, but he was too hardheaded to listen.

"You wanna go chill by Uncle Bryce with your cousins for a little while?" Jaden asked his daughter.

"Yes!" Jaylynn shouted. "Can I bring the snacks over there too?"

"Yeah, pack it up while I go put some clothes on," Jaden replied.

He threw on a pair of Levi's jeans with the matching t-shirt and slipped his feet in a pair of Air Max. Jaden wondered if Tigga knew what Keller's sneaky ass was up to. He was about to call and put him up on game, just in case he didn't.

"What's up bruh?" Tigga said when he answered the phone.

"Where did Keller tell you that she was going?" Jaden asked, getting right to the point.

"Out for drinks with your girl and my sister," Tigga replied.

"Their sneaky asses went to Co-Co's freaky stripper party," Jaden informed him.

"Oh yeah?" Tigga questioned uncaringly.

"Fuck you mean, oh yeah? You cool with that shit?"

"Nigga, we been hitting the strip club damn near every week for a month. I'm not about to trip on my girl for going to no stripper party."

"We go there for business though. They on some other shit. And Kia straight up lied to me about where she was going. Her sneaky ass changed clothes and everything. Got that short, tight ass dress on with them high ass heels. I'm bout' to go up in that bitch and act a fool. You rollin'?" Jaden asked.

"Fuck no," Tigga replied. "My kids are with their mama this weekend, and I'm sippin' and smokin' until my girl gets home."

"Man, come make that run with me. I wouldn't leave you hanging like that. They might fuck around and jump me if I go by myself," Jaden argued.

"Nigga, I just told you that I been drinking. I'm not getting behind the wheel of no car," Tigga replied.

"Don't trip, I'll be there in ten," Jaden said, right before he hung up. He made sure that his daughter had everything that she needed before they hopped in his car and were on their way.

Chapter 10

"Get it Kia bitch!" Co-Co yelled as he rained dollars all over her. Kia was feeling herself something serious. She had been getting her drink on and she quickly became the life of the party. Co-Co and his friend, Sweets, had the entire club lit. The stage that was usually occupied by the drag queens who performed was now being used by the strippers to entertain the party guests. Kia had been up on the stage most of the night and Co-Co was happy to see her having fun. Being with a man like Jaden had to be stressful and Kia needed to let her hair down and unwind.

"That bitch is drunk out of her mind!" Keller yelled over the music.

"She sure is and I love it," Co-Co replied.

"She better slow down with the liquor. Jaden is gonna die if she goes home drunk like that," Keller acknowledged.

"Fuck Jaden! Let my girl do her," Co-Co said. "Y'all come in the back with me and help me get some more food."

"Baby, y'all did the damn thing, but where the hell did y'all find all of these strippers?" Tessa questioned when they got to a quieter area in the back of the club.

"Bitch, I got the juice. When Co-Co calls, they all come running. And I heard you got a new man Tessa. You be in everybody else's mix, but you forgot to mention that bit of info," Co-Co said, calling her out.

"She don't like my friend, but I don't know why. Ryan is a good dude," Keller butted in.

"I do like him, but he's too much of a mama's boy for me. He broke our very first date because his mama claimed that she wasn't feeling well. He's starting out bad already." Tessa frowned.

"Baby girl, I can't agree with you on that one. I wish my mama was here for me to cater to her. I love Lisa with all my heart, but you only get one mother," Co-Co said, speaking of his father's wife. She came into their lives not too long ago, but she quickly earned a spot in him and Candace's hearts. Co-Co and Candace were both adults, but Lisa treated them like they were her little babies.

"It's not just that. His mama don't like me. He took me over there for dinner to meet her and his sisters, and she was acting like a real bitch. His sisters were nice and talked to me, but she just kept rolling her eyes like a lil ass girl," Tessa said.

"Ms. Emily is sweet. Ryan is her baby, so she's probably just a little overprotective. Things are still new with y'all. Just give it some time," Keller suggested.

"Bitch, you're already in. You met the family and everything. Give it time, like Keller said. If it's still not sweet after a few months, then do what you have to do," Co-Co replied.

"If you feel like it's too much to deal with, then bounce." Keller shrugged.

"Look at you, giving out advice and shit. Did your man ever catch up with fright night?" he said, referring to Leo.

"Nope and I hope he never does. I don't want Tigga going to jail or getting hurt over that bullshit. Leo gon' get everything that he deserves and more. With his ugly ass." Keller frowned.

"Oh, now you can see that he's ugly. Nigga been walking round her looking like he got on a costume all year round and you just now noticing it. And then, he got the nerve to bring a child into the world. Poor lil boy look just like the black Benjamin Button," Co-Co said, making them laugh as they followed him back out carrying more food to the table.

By then, the stage was cleared and Sweets was on the microphone introducing the final act of the night. All of the dancers had their routines put together and a few of them just walked around dancing randomly. Kia was back in her seat at the front near the stage with Brooklyn and Candace, so Co-Co, Keller, and Tessa walked up there to join them.

"You good sis?" Keller asked once she sat down next to her.

"Bitch, I'm great." Kia smiled as she fanned herself with a few napkins.

"Drunk ass," Brooklyn laughed and teased her.

"I'm not drunk, but I feel damn good. These strippers are fine as hell!" Kia yelled.

"Bitch, don't even think about it. Most of them are probably gay, which explains how Co-Co and Sweets know them," Candace replied.

"Most of them are but not all. Let me show you the straight ones. Now, pay attention because it's not that many," Co-Co said as he pointed out two men who were out working the crowd. One, in particular, kept pulling Kia up on the stage all night, so she had to know about him. He kept grabbing at her ass, but that didn't mean a thing.

"What about him Co-Co?" Kia asked, pointing to the man who kept his eyes on her all night.

"Oh, he's straight and a straight up hoe," Co-Co replied, right as the man went to the back with a few of the other dancers.

A few minutes later, the lights went out and sirens could be heard going off all around the room. The flickering lights on the stage illuminated the room enough for everybody to see what was going on. The women in attendance went wild when five dancers came to the stage dressed in police uniforms. Kia's boy toy for the night was the first to come out and his eyes landed directly on hers.

"Aww shit Kia. Your boo thang is coming back for you. You might be under arrest," Candace and Brooklyn teased. Just like they assumed, Kia's new love interest danced his way right over to them. Instead of pulling Kia up on the stage like he usually did, he left her right where she was and started dancing in front of her. He kept his eyes fixated on hers as he removed every article of clothing, with the exception of the flap that covered his genital area.

"What's your name?" he whispered in Kia's ear.

"Kia. What's yours?" she replied.

"Darrius, but my stage name is Cock Diesel. You wanna know why?" he flirted.

"Hell yeah, I do." Kia smiled up at him.

He grabbed her small hand and placed it on his chest. Kia was nervous, but she giggled with anticipation as he guided her hand further down towards his midsection. He had a cocky smirk on his face as he watched her watching him. Kia knew that he was working with something because the print in his uniform left little to the imagination. Her first mind told her to stop him but, the lower he guided her hand, the more curious she became. Kia closed her eyes, waiting for her hand to make contact with his most prized possession, but that never happened.

"I wish the fuck you would!" Jaden roared as he grabbed the stripper's arm and twisted it behind his back. He lifted his shirt to reveal his gun, just in case the other man wanted to get courageous. Kia's eyes popped open and all of her senses came rushing back to her at once when she heard his voice.

"Wh... what are you doing here?" she stuttered as she turned to face Jaden's angry face.

"Nah, the question is, what the fuck are you doing here? Whatever happened to dinner and drinks with Keller and Tessa?" he fumed.

"We decided to come here instead," Kia replied.

"That's bullshit Kia. You had this shit planned from the jump. Your sneaky ass had changing clothes and everything. Get your shit and let's go. Don't make me go off up in this bitch. And your musty ass better get the fuck on before you become a casualty of war," Jaden said to the stripper, who was still standing there like a dummy.

The lights came back on and the DJ cut the music as soon as it looked like an altercation was about to take place. People had already started heading for the exit before things got too far out of hand.

"Y'all sit back down. It's cool; this is my cousin. He ain't gon' do nothing!" Co-Co yelled, trying to ease everyone's minds. "Don't come in here trying to ruin my damn party Jaden. You get on my nerves with that shit."

"You better sit your ass down somewhere looking like a fucking laundry bag," he said, cracking on the all-black mesh shirt that Co-Co had on.

"Oh no you didn't, bitch! This is a two-hundred-dollar shirt honey. Don't get me started in here Jaden. I'm warming you." Co-Co rolled his eyes.

"All y'all muthafuckers going straight to hell and Co-Co gon' be the ring leader. Got it looking just like Sodom and Gomorrah up in here. Let's go Kia!" Jaden barked angrily.

"Nigga, don't holler at me. I'm coming!" Kia yelled back.

"And what the hell are you laughing at Tigga?" Keller said as she pulled him out of the club behind her sister and Jaden.

"Y'all got a straight up freak fest going on in this bitch," he said, cracking up.

"Where is your truck?" Keller asked, once they made it out front.

"That nigga Jaden picked me up. I'm riding back with y'all," Tigga replied. They heard Kia and Jaden arguing all throughout the parking lot, but that was nothing new.

"Is Kia straight?" Tessa questioned.

"She's good. This ain't nothing new," Keller replied. She knew that, as crazy as Jaden was, he would never lay a finger on her sister.

"Aye, come sit back here with me," Tigga said while pulling Keller towards the back door of Tessa's car.

"Hell no, she will not!" Tessa yelled. "Y'all better save that shit for when y'all get home. I ain't never seen nobody fuck as much as y'all do."

"Ole hating ass," Tigga said as he got into the car. Keller looked good as hell in her lil black dress and he couldn't wait to get her inside.

***

"You got niggas whispering in your ear and shit. Feeling all on his dick!" Jaden yelled as he towered over Kia.

"I was not feeling on that man's dick," Kia said as she rubbed her temples.

"Only because I stopped your hot ass," Jaden replied.

"Jaden chill out, please. I have a headache," Kia begged as she stood to her feet.

They had been home for over an hour and had been arguing off and on since then. Kia grabbed the bag of clothes that she took to Mo's house and started putting everything away.

"I don't give a fuck about your headache. That's what your lying ass get for drinking. Nasty ass niggas slanging their dicks all in your face," Jaden continued to fuss.

"The same way those nasty hoes be poppin' their pussies all in your face. Don't try to go off on me when you be in the strip club just about every weekend. Keller already told me, so don't even fix your mouth to tell a lie!" Kia yelled.

Jaden could have choked Tigga for telling Keller everything. They were on that open, honest relationship shit, but he took it too far sometimes. He couldn't take a piss without sending Keller a text.

"That's only for business. Your hot ass was just being sneaky," Jaden countered.

"Whatever Jaden. I'm tired and I'm going to bed," Kia said as she removed her wedge heels from the bag and attempted to put them in the closet.

"You can go to bed when we finish talking," Jaden said, grabbing her arm.

"Talk to yourself, I'm done." Kia yawned, pissing Jaden off.

He hated when she ignored him, but she just wasn't in the mood to continue their conversation. He had been following her all over the house fussing and she was over it. He even stood outside of the shower, going off about the same stupid thing.

"Don't play with me, Kia!" Jaden yelled as he turned her around to face him.

"Move!" Kia snapped as she turned around and hit him in the eye with the heel of her shoe.

"Ahh! Fuck!" Jaden yelled while dropping to the floor, holding his eye.

"Oh shit! Baby, I'm so sorry. It was an accident," Kia said while dropping down to the floor to see about him.

"You beating on a nigga now Kia?" Jaden asked as he continued to cradle his throbbing orb.

"No baby, I'm so sorry. Let me get you some ice," Kia said while getting up and running to the kitchen.

"Bitch trying to kill me," Jaden mumbled once she was gone. His eye felt like it had a pulse, so he knew that it would probably be swollen or worse.

"Here, let me see it," Kia insisted when she came back into the room. Jaden was sitting with his back against the wall, so she crawled in between his legs. Once she moved his hand, she replaced it with the ice pack that she had just come back with.

"That shit is burning," Jaden moaned in agony.

"I know, I'm sorry," Kia apologized again. "You want me to kiss it?"

"Yep," Jaden said, sounding like a big ass baby.

"Okay," Kia said as she removed the ice pack and gave his aching eye a kiss.

"I love you," Jaden said as they sat on the floor and cuddled.

"I love you too," Kia replied with a smile.

And just like that, the events of the night were forgotten. That's how it always was and would probably always be. Everybody knew that their relationship was dysfunctional, but it was perfectly normal to the two of them.

Chapter 11

Anaya sat outside in her car fuming mad, as she dialed Tigga's number. They had gone to their final court hearing for child support two weeks prior and she had just gotten her letter stating how much she was being awarded every month. She originally asked for three thousand dollars per child, but her legal aid lawyer convinced her to go down just a little. Since Tigga paid the rent and they shared custody of the kids, she agreed to the sum of five thousand dollars per month. That was twenty-five hundred per child and still enough for her to live comfortably. Tigga had paid the rent up for six months, but she knew that once he found out that Rich was staying there, he wouldn't be doing it anymore. She was sure that her daughters were going to tell him, if they hadn't already. Her hopes of having enough money to live on went tumbling down in a matter of seconds. Anaya was heated when she read the letter informing her that she would only be receiving twelve hundred per child, totaling twenty-four hundred a month. That was two pairs of shoes for Tigga, so that wasn't shit in his eyes. The rent on the place that she was living in was half of that, so she would probably have to move. Not to mention, all of the utilities and her car insurance. Anaya was no longer working, so there was no way that she could live off of that small sum of money. Tigga had a multi-million-dollar company and he should have been ordered to pay much more.

"Are you fucking serious Tigga? Twenty-four hundred dollars? What the fuck am I supposed to do with that shit?" Anaya yelled when he answered the phone.

"You better budget and make that shit work," he said like he didn't have a care in the world.

"Nigga, you got jokes? I bet you spend more than that every month on that bitch Keller!" Anaya screamed.

"Don't worry about Keller. You were the one who went to the courts begging for child support. I take care of my kids. Your bitter ass just wanted money for yourself. Now, the rent and everything else is all on you. As long as my kids are straight, I don't give a fuck about what happens to you. Tell your other baby daddy to help you out."

"You don't give a damn about your kids. You know I can't afford to pay that high ass rent and all of the bills on my own."

"Not my problem. You can give me full custody of my kids if you can't handle it though. Me and my girl would be happy to have them."

"Nigga, fuck you and your girl. She ain't playing mama to my kids. And tell that stupid, uppity hoe to keep her hands out of my girls' heads. Bitch can't comb hair to save her life!" Anaya yelled before she hung up the phone.

She ended her conversation just in time to see Rich come walking out of the building. He looked nice in his slacks and button down shirt and tie. His hair was freshly cut and lined to perfection.

"Let's roll," he said when he got into the car and snatched off his clip on tie.

"What happened?" Anaya asked while looking over at him.

"Same shit, different day. They always said they gon' call, but they never do. Nobody wants to hire a convicted felon." Rich shrugged like he was used to the treatment.

He had been job hunting hard for over a month, but nothing had come through for him yet. Anaya was getting fed up with him always being broke, but he really was trying to do something about it.

"Now what?" Anaya questioned.

"I just have to keep looking. I told you that I won't stop until I find something," he promised.

"Well, I have another problem, but what's new?" Anaya said, showing him the letter from the child support office.

"Twenty-four hundred dollars?" Rich yelled excitedly. "You call this a problem? That's damn good if you ask me."

"Good!" Anaya yelled. "That lil money can't do shit for me. You can't be serious. I'm used to living a certain way and this ain't it."

"Stop acting brand new girl. You grew up in the trailer park just like me. That nigga introduced you to the lavish life and now you act like you can't do without it. I'm telling you right now, I can't afford to do half of what he did, so please don't be expecting it. I wanna be able to provide and keep a roof over your head, but I'm a simple nigga," Rich said honestly.

"So, you want me to lower my standards? Is that what you're saying?"

"So, being with me is lowering your standards?" Rich questioned, feeling slightly hurt by her words.

"Don't put words in my mouth Rich," Anaya said, trying to smooth things over.

"No, you said it, so own up to it. I'm trying, but I can't promise you anything more than that. Don't string me along and waste my time if I'm not what you want Anaya. I allowed you to do that long enough."

"Can we not do this right now Rich?" Anaya begged.

"No, let's do this shit right here, right now. Let's keep it real Anaya. Without your kids' daddy paying the rent on that place, we'll probably have to move to a more affordable one soon. The shopping and shit that you love so much is going to be limited now. I'm not breaking my back trying to live in another man's shadow," Rich said seriously.

"I'm not asking you to Amir," she said, calling him by his real name. "I just want both of us to have a job and take care of each other. I don't want to be the sole bread winner in the household."

"And you won't be. I promised you that I'd do my part and I will. I'm trying to do things the legal way, but nothing is coming through. I might have to hit the block again, just to get some money flowing in," he replied, making Anaya cringe.

Rich just didn't understand that being a dope boy wasn't for him. He tried and failed too many times to count. Anaya didn't want to kick him while he was down, so she decided to keep her comments to herself. She had enough on her plate and she refused to let Rich add to her stress. She would take his word for now, but only time would tell if he made good on his promises.

Chapter 12

"Fuck!" Tigga yelled as he held Keller up, pumping in and out of her wetness. She had her legs wrapped around his waist, while he held her up against the bathroom door.

"Ssh, your kids are right there in the room," Keller whispered as she covered his mouth with her hand.

"I'm trying, but I can't help it," Tigga replied while burying his face in her neck. Keller was just getting out of the shower when he slipped into the bathroom with her for a quickie.

"Hurry up baby. Tessa's gonna be waiting on me to pick her up," Keller mumbled as she enjoyed the feel of him hitting her spot once again.

She bit her bottom lip to keep from screaming out, as another orgasm overtook her body. She almost lost her senses when Tigga gripped her waist tighter and started going faster. Keller bit his shoulder and shut her eyes tight as the feeling became too much for her to bear.

"Damn baby! Ahh, shit!" Tigga yelled as he came hard, making him feel like he wanted to collapse.

"Boy, you better not drop me," Keller said as she held on to his neck.

"Girl, that took a lot out of me. I need a nap after that one," Tigga said as he walked her over to the shower.

He and Keller washed up quickly and snuck back into the bedroom, while his daughters were still focused on the television.

"Are we still going by our grandma Keller?" Tia asked while staring at the cartoons on the tv screen.

"Yeah, you and Talia come on, so I can comb y'all hair," Keller replied.

Christy was off from work, so she wanted her granddaughters to spend a few hours at her house. She was cooking a huge pot of gumbo, so she invited her kids and Keller over as well. Tigga didn't feel like going, so he made his mother promise to send him some food home with Keller.

"Can Amari come too?" Tia asked, looking over at her father.

"I don't know baby. I think she's with her nanny," Tigga replied, trying to keep from telling her the truth.

Anaya had been in her feelings a lot lately. She was mad because she would eventually have to move into a new apartment and she blamed Tigga for no longer paying the rent on the old one. She had a man living with her, but she wanted Tigga to take care of her because she was the mother of his kids. She had a baby with that other nigga too, but he obviously wasn't handling his business. She was being petty and decided that Amari couldn't come over to his house with the other girls anymore. She claimed that her man was tired of Amari thinking that Tigga was her father. That was cool with him, but he knew that Amari probably didn't understand what was happening.

"Your grandma got y'all a pool, so make sure to bring y'all bathing suits," Keller said, trying hard to change the subject. She was happy that it worked because the girls jumped up and ran to their room to retrieve their swim suits.

"You do know that Anaya is picking them up from my mama's house, right?" Tigga asked Keller, once the girls were gone.

"Yeah," she replied while searching through the girls' hair supplies to find bows to match their outfits.

"Let my mama deal with her, Keller. I don't need you and Tessa on no bullshit with that crazy ass girl," Tigga lectured.

"I don't have anything to say to Anaya. She has a problem with me, not the other way around. That bitch be acting like we were friends and I stole her man. She never did like me, so I don't see what the issue is," Keller argued.

"I know baby, but just do what I'm asking you. For the sake of my kids, I want everything to remain peaceful," Tigga replied while Keller rolled her eyes upward. She was happy when the girls came back into the room because she was tired of talking about his trifling ass baby mama.

Tigga went into the living room to watch the sports channel, while Keller got his girls ready to go. He had been in the office a lot more than usual lately and he wanted to take the entire day to relax and do nothing. He wished Keller could stay inside with him, but he would be able to chill with her later. About thirty minutes later, both of his daughters walked into the room and sat on the sofa next to him. Tigga had to keep himself from laughing when he looked at their hair. Keller was really trying, but his babies' hair was a hot ass mess. After a while, he couldn't hold it in any longer and fell out laughing. His daughters were looking at him like he was crazy, but he would never tell them what he was laughing at.

"What's wrong with you?" Keller asked when she walked into the room.

"Nothing," Tigga said, trying hard to suppress his smile. Keller saw him looking at his daughters' hair, so she already knew what he was snickering at.

"Ugh, you make me sick. At least I tried," she said before walking off to the bedroom with Tigga following right behind her.

"Stop being so damn emotional girl. You did alright," he said, turning his head so she wouldn't see that he was still laughing.

"Is it really that bad?" Keller asked, laughing with him.

"Oh, it's fucked up, no doubt about it, but I appreciate you for trying," he said sincerely.

"I can't comb hair for shit. That's why Kia always made sure to get braids in Jaylynn's hair whenever she stayed a few days with me. Maybe I need to make them an appointment with Candace. That's who braids my niece's hair," Keller replied.

"Yeah, make that shit ASAP," Tigga urged.

"Shut up Tigga. I'll call her and do it later. We're about to go, give me a kiss," Keller said, walking away from him.

"I love you," Tigga said before pecking her on her lips.

"Love you too," Keller said before getting the girls and walking out of the house.

A few hours later, she and Tessa were relaxing with Christy in her backyard. They were all full as ticks after eating several bowls of the gumbo that she had prepared. The girls were in their pool having fun, while the three of them sat around and talked.

"So, what's up with you and Ryan? He seems like a sweetheart," Christy said to her daughter.

"He is, but Tessa is just mean," Keller butted in.

"I'm not mean and nothing is up with us. That nigga must have been a breastfed baby. He can't seem to get off the titty," Tessa spat.

"No you did not just say that," Keller said as she and Christy laughed.

"I'm serious though girl. We went to the movies the other night, and his mama must have called ten times in two hours. He thought it was an emergency, but her needy ass only wanted him to bring her something to eat." Tessa frowned.

"Did he do it?" Christy asked.

"Does Al Sharpton have a perm?" Tessa retorted, making them laugh again.

"Girl, you are too stupid." Keller continued to chuckle.

"And, then, when we got there, his sisters were already over there. I was wondering why she couldn't have asked one of them to go get her something to eat. Better yet, why couldn't she have gone to get it herself?" Tessa questioned.

"So, now what? You don't like him no more because of that?" Keller asked.

"Yeah, I still like him, but I just decided to fall back for a while. I'm not trying to compete with nobody's mama. I've been single for a minute and I don't mind continuing," Tessa replied.

Keller only nodded her head because she agreed with what her friend was saying. Ryan was a good catch for any woman, but his mama was going to always be his problem. Keller used to joke and tell him that his mama treated him like he was her man, but that was really the truth. She never asked him what happened with his ex-girlfriend, but she was sure that Ms. Emily had a lot to do with the break-up. Keller made a mental note to talk to her boy about what was going on. She would hate to see him and Tessa call it quits before giving their relationship a fair try. She knew in her heart that they would be good together. They just had to see it for themselves.

"Y'all can leave if y'all want to. It's getting late and there's no telling what time Anaya is going to pick them up," Christy said after they talked for a while.

"And your son is blowing my phone up for his food," Keller said, standing to her feet.

"Tell him that there's plenty more if he wants it. I made a huge pot of it. I have to send his grandparents some too," Christy replied.

She didn't want to leave her granddaughters in the pool, so she asked Keller and Tessa to see themselves out. Tessa had a key, so that wasn't a problem. Once she and Keller grabbed their containers of food, Tessa locked the door and they headed to Keller's truck. Once they pulled off and turned the corner, Tessa began to search for her phone. She knew that it was in her purse, but she couldn't find that either.

"Girl, I think I left my purse at my mama's house," Tessa said as she continued to look around the truck.

"That's a damn shame. Your greedy ass didn't forget that gumbo though," Keller laughed as she made the block and headed back to Christy's house.

"I'll be right back," Tessa said as she jumped out of the truck and ran up the walkway.

"Bring me back a bottle of water!" Keller rolled down the window and yelled.

She reached in the back seat and grabbed her phone out of her purse. Tigga was probably going crazy wondering where his food was and she needed to put his mind at ease. She laughed when she got the phone because she had a missed call and a text message from him already.

"Where you at?" he questioned as soon as she called him back.

"On my wa... ahhh!!" Keller's words were cut short when somebody reached into the window of her car and grabbed her hair.

She heard Tigga asking her what was wrong, but her phone fell from her hand as soon as she was grabbed. Whoever it was, was trying to pull her out of the truck through the window and they were almost succeeding. Her seatbelt being connected was the only thing keeping her in place. Keller thought sure that it was Leo attacking her again, until she heard Anaya's ghetto ass voice.

"Bitch, I told you that I would see you again. You thought I was playing hoe?" Anaya said as she repeatedly punched Keller in her face and head. The iron taste in her mouth let Keller know that she was bleeding. She was angry that she couldn't really defend herself because Anaya was beating the hell out of her. The seatbelt kept her from being pulled out of the truck, but it also hindered her from being able to fight back. Keller swore that if she could get to her glove box, she was going to shoot Anaya right in the face.

"No this bitch is not fighting my friend!" Keller heard Tessa yell.

Anaya stopped attacking Keller almost immediately and she saw why. Tessa and Anaya were in a full blown mix in a matter of seconds. Keller didn't think twice as she took off her seatbelt and got out to help her friend. The two of them were hitting every part of Anaya's body that was visible and she was having a hard time trying to keep up. Anaya had some serious hands and none of them could dispute that. Keller was pulling her hair and punching her in the face, the same way she'd done her a few minutes ago. She was so thankful for Tessa coming to her rescue because she would have been in a world of trouble if she didn't. The more Keller thought about it, the angrier she became. She backed away from the fight and ran to her truck. After opening her glove box, she grabbed her pink and wood grain gun and attempted to walk back over to the fight.

"Let me go!" Keller screamed when she was lifted off of her feet and carried back towards her truck.

"Girl, calm your ass down! Give me this damn gun," Tigga roared as he snatched the weapon from her hand. He was already on his way over there, since Keller was taking so long with his food. As soon as he heard her yelling on the phone, he broke the speed limit getting to Christy's house as fast as he could. Christy had run outside and pulled Tessa and Anaya apart a few seconds later. She looked out of her window and saw them fighting, but she wanted to make sure that her granddaughters didn't witness it. Unfortunately, they were both standing on the porch crying and watching as everything unfolded.

"Tessa, stop!" Christy yelled while pulling her daughter away from her grandkids' mother. "Your nieces don't need to see that shit."

"Y'all weak hoes had to jump me. You ain't got no hands bitch!" Anaya yelled as she ran up on Keller again.

"You better get the fuck on Anaya," Tigga said as he pushed her away. He didn't mean to push her to the ground, but she went tumbling down to the concrete anyway.

"You putting your hands on me in front of my kids for this bitch, Tigga. This hoe got you that far gone!" Anaya yelled as she continued to try to get at Keller.

"I'm calling the police if you don't get away from my house Anaya. Look at what you're doing to your kids," Christy said with tears in her eyes. She hated that her grandkids were put in the middle of their mess because it wasn't fair to them.

"Give me my gun!" Keller screamed while punching Tigga in his back. "I'm about to shoot this bitch right in her forehead."

"Calm. The. Fuck. Down!!" Tigga said through gritted teeth. Keller was losing her damn mind, talking about killing somebody like it was normal. She was starting to make him regret even getting the gun for her. The gun was supposed to be for her protection, but she was on some crazy shit at the moment.

"You taking up for your baby mama now Tyler," Keller accused.

"Don't be stupid Keller. You standing here talking about killing my kids' mama and they're standing right there watching you. The fuck is you on right now?" he barked, shocking Keller with his hostile tone.

"Fuck you, nigga! And fuck your baby mama drama. I'm over this shit," Keller said as she backed up and went back to her truck. Tessa ran over and hopped in the front seat, right before Keller sped away from the madness. Tigga was heated about how everything went down. As bad as he wanted to go after Keller, he had to make sure that his kids were okay first.

"Give me my kids, so I can get the fuck away from here," Anaya spat angrily.

"You not taking my kids nowhere. And if you don't want me to knock you the fuck out, you better take your stupid ass on somewhere. You look pathetic as fuck out here fighting in front of them," Tigga replied with fire in his eyes.

He was waiting for Anaya to say something flip but, to his surprise, she turned around and walked back to her truck. Christy had calmed the girls down and took them inside, but he wanted to talk to them as well. It felt like he just couldn't have one drama free weekend. First, it was Jaden and Kia last week; now, it was him and Keller with problems the next. Tigga sighed in aggravation as she entered his mother's house and prepared to talk to his kids.

Chapter 13

Keller was happy to be back at work the following Tuesday after she and Tigga had it out. He had been calling her like crazy, but she had no words for him. It wasn't his fault that Anaya attacked her, but she was still pissed about how he talked to her in front of his ex. She had been staying by Kia's house since that Sunday night and they hadn't seen each other since then. Jaden was on her back about going back home, but she wasn't trying to hear him. Nobody could tell him anything about his relationship with Kia and Keller felt the same way.

"Baby, I wish I was out there when that bitch put her hands on you. You are too pretty to be walking around here with scratches and bruises on your face," Co-Co vented to Keller as he curled his customer's hair.

"She caught me off guard. I'm not saying that I would have won the fight if she didn't, but at least I would have been prepared," Keller replied as she polished her customer's nails.

"Have you been putting the aloe on your face like I told you to?" Co-Co asked.

"Yeah, that's why it's clearing up so fast," Keller replied.

"It is clearing up fast. That's what I told this jackass, but he don't like to listen," Co-Co said, pointing at Jaden.

Jaden was walking around with a broken blood vessel in his black eye, as a result of Kia hitting him with a shoe. He claimed it was an accident, but none of them were trying to hear him.

"Mind your damn business. Don't worry about my eye," Jaden said as he sat in his barber's chair, waiting for Dwight.

He was Jaden's first customer of the day, but he stopped to get lunch for everyone before he came. Dwight was such a sweetheart and Keller often wondered how he hooked up with Co-Co's crazy ass. The saying that opposites attract was definitely true because they were nothing alike.

"Nigga, I was trying to help you out. Black eyes matter," Co-Co said, making everybody laugh. It was even funnier because Jaden was wearing his black lives matter t-shirt at the time.

"You laughing and shit, but when are you bringing your ass back home?" Jaden said, turning the conversation on Keller.

"I'm getting my own house. I'm sick of staying with niggas and be running from house to house when shit go left," Keller replied.

"I know that's right Keller. Get your own shit, so you can send them niggas on their way," Co-Co agreed.

"You would be a damn fool to take advice from a nigga that pepper sprayed himself." Jaden frowned.

"And she would be an even bigger fool to listen to a nigga who gets beat on by his girlfriend," Co-Co shot back.

"Y'all chill out. We got customers." Keller laughed.

"I'm just saying though Keller. My boy really loves you. He didn't even do nothing wrong for you to be doing him like that. He can't control what his baby mama does," Jaden replied.

"I know that, but I didn't appreciate him talking to me crazy in front of that bitch either."

"You were talking about shooting the damn girl in front of her kids. You was out of your mind with that shit," Jaden scolded.

Keller only nodded her head, as she put the finishing touches on her client's nails. She knew that she had gone too far when she was talking about shooting Anaya, but her anger overtook all of her other emotions. It was a good thing that Tigga took the gun from her because she was really ready to pull the trigger.

"I'll see you in two weeks Keller," her customer said before she got up and headed for the door.

"Where is Dwight? I have thirty minutes before my big crowd comes in," Keller announced.

"What big crowd? Tuesday's are usually slow days. What's going on in the city like that?" Co-Co asked.

"I don't know, but some lady booked me up for the rest of the day. She paid her deposit online, so I'm good either way," Keller replied, right as Dwight walked in the shop carrying bags of food. He was right on time for her to eat and relax before she got really busy.

"What's up y'all?" he said, speaking to everybody.

"Don't let them touch nothing until I get my food out," Co-Co ordered as he sprayed oil sheen on his customer's finished hair.

"You must be crazy. I'm getting my shit out right now," Jaden said, standing to his feet.

"Now I see why Kia blackened your eye. Your ass is too hardheaded," Co-Co fussed.

"Chill out Co-Co. I got your stuff separate from everybody else's," Dwight said calmly.

"My boo knows me so well." Co-Co blushed.

Jaden and Keller ignored him, as they fixed their food and sat down to eat. Jaden had been asking her and Brooklyn to help him pick Kia out a ring and she was too excited to do it. Jaden and Kia had been together forever, so marriage was long overdue. They both continued to make small talk long after they had finished eating. Keller's client was running a little late, but she was enjoying the break. When the door chimed, she looked up expecting to see a group of women come in. Her face twisted up into a frown instead, when she locked eyes with an unwanted visitor.

"Tigga, my nigga." Jaden smiled as he stood up to greet him with a handshake. Tigga shook his hand, but he kept his focus on Keller the entire time.

"How everybody doing?" Tigga asked with his gaze still burning a hole through Keller. She ignored him and pretended to play with her fingernails.

"Stop being so damn childish and speak to that man," Jaden ordered.

"Mind your business," Keller snapped at him.

"Let me talk to you for a minute," Tigga said while tapping Keller on her leg.

"I can't, I'm waiting for my customers," Keller replied.

"I don't see nobody here yet," Tigga said, looking around the shop.

"They're running late, but I'm booked up for the rest of the day. I'll call you later," Keller said, trying to get him to leave her alone.

"Who are you waiting for, Maria Givens?" Tigga smirked, making Keller snap her head around in his direction.

"How do you know that?" Keller questioned. Maria Givens was the lady who made the appointment and filled up her schedule for the entire day, but Tigga would have never figured that out unless somebody told him.

"My bad for being late, but I'm here," he said, making everybody laugh with the exception of Keller.

"Are you fucking serious! I'm missing out on money because you feel like playing these childish ass games!" Keller yelled angrily.

"Shut up and let me talk to you," Tigga said as he pulled her out of the chair and towards the storage room in the back of the shop.

"I turned down customers who wanted to come in today because I thought I was gonna be booked up. This shit is not funny Tigga," Keller said as soon as he closed the door.

"I'm not laughing. If you would have talked to me when I was begging you to, I wouldn't have had to go through all of this. And don't even fix your mouth to say shit to me about money. I got plenty of that, so don't insult me," Tigga fussed.

"You still could have found a better way to get at me than this. You could have called."

"How? Your damn phone is off again," Tigga fussed.

"It is?" Keller replied while pulling it from her back pocket.

"All of that is irrelevant Keller. I'm here now and you're free for the day. I'm honestly trying to see what you're upset about. I should be the one pissed about how y'all carried on in front of my kids."

"I apologize for that, but I didn't appreciate how you talked to be in front of your baby mama. If you wanted to check me about anything, you should have done that shit at another place and time. That bitch attacked me and you went off like I was wrong."

"I never said that you were wrong for defending yourself, but pulling out a gun was taking shit too far. I got you that gun for protection, not to pull it out every time somebody piss you off. Nobody even considered my kids who were standing there watching everything go down. You know how hard it was for me to have to sit down and explain that shit to them."

Keller dropped her head, feeling bad for the part that she played in everything. She was wrong to some extent and she had no problem admitting that. It was crazy how she got mad and was ready to leave Tigga over something so small, but she took Leo's bullshit for years and stayed with his dog ass.

"I gotta do better," she mumbled loud enough for him to hear.

"Yeah, you do," Tigga replied as he pulled her in for a hug.

"I know, I'm sorry," Keller said, hugging him back.

"I accept that, now bring your ass back home," he replied with a smile.

"I will." Keller smiled back.

"And you need to get better with your bills too Keller. I don't understand how you forget to pay your shit. You forgot your car note last month and now your phone is off," Tigga fussed.

"I know," Keller replied.

She wasn't used to paying her own bills because Leo took care of everything when they were together. When they broke up, she switched cellphone providers, but she kept her same phone number. Aside from her booth rental that she paid Bryce, she was always late or forgot to pay everything else. Tigga was always telling her that she was ruining her credit, but that still wasn't enough to make her do better.

"Why won't you just let me pay the truck off? It's in your name, so it's not like I can take it from you," Tigga offered.

"No Tigga, you already pay the insurance on it. I think I'm gonna set it up at the bank where they automatically take it out on the first of every month. That way I won't have to worry about being late again."

"I hear your stubborn ass," he replied, shaking his head. "Let's go."

"Go where?" Keller questioned.

"You're done for the rest of the day. Let's go home," he replied.

"I'm only done because of your ass." She laughed.

"I got you," Tigga said as he pulled a huge knot of money from his front pocket.

"No baby, I'm just messing with you. Put your money away," Keller told him.

"I'm trying to give you a chance to earn it. You off from the shop, but you can put in some work at home if you want to," Tigga said with a wink.

"Hell yeah. You can be ready to go broke today nigga." Keller laughed.

She grabbed her purse and told everybody that she was leaving for the day. Tigga was flaunting his money in her face, but he was about to lose every penny of it. Keller had a few tricks up her sleeve that she was ready to use on him. It had been a few days since they had been intimate and she was in need. She and Tigga had sex just about every day, so she was sure that he was feeling the same way.

Chapter 14

"If you don't have your shit out of my house today, it's going out with the trash tomorrow!" Toni yelled to her sister Tori over the phone.

"Bitch, you throw my shit out and we gon' have a problem," Tori replied.

"Think I'm playing if you want to. I can't have niggas kicking my door down behind your bullshit. I got kids and my landlord don't play that. I don't know what you did and I don't care. Come get your shit out of my house and don't even worry about visiting me no more!" Toni yelled right before she hung up the phone in her face.

"What did she say?" Anna questioned.

"She wants my stuff out of her house. That bitch know that I don't have nowhere else to go," Tori said, wiping tears from her eyes.

Tori had been sleeping from house to house for the past few months, but she didn't have a steady place to live. Her mother let her stay a few nights over there but, as soon as her man said something about it, Tori had to go. It had always been that way with her, so Tori wasn't surprised. She knew that she was putting her sister and her kids at risk when she attacked Kia, but she did it anyway. Jaden had kicked in Toni's door twice since then and she was scared out of her mind. Toni couldn't afford to move, so she had to stay there and look over her shoulder every day and night. She lost count of how many people Jaden had sent there to look for Tori, and she was sick and tired of it.

"You knew that when you went after that girl. You said yourself that her boyfriend was crazy. I only have a two-bedroom trailer, so I can't help you with a place to stay," Anna informed her before she even asked. She didn't even know Jaden and she was scared of him. Just by hearing the stories that Tori told, she knew that he wasn't one to be played with. Tori liked to play with fire and she always ended up getting burned.

"Did I ask you for a place to stay?" Tori snapped in anger.

"I was just putting it out there. Don't get mad with me. You need to ask Donna if you can crash by her for a while," Anna said, referring to her own mother.

"I don't wanna live in no damn trailer park," Tori said with a frown. "I just need somewhere to keep my stuff."

"Well, excuse the hell out of me. It's a lot better than living on the streets. My mama lives alone, so she's probably your only hope. It ain't like Darlene give a fuck about you having a place to sleep," Anna said, referring to Tori's mother. It was a known fact that Darlene put the men in her life above all else, including her kids and grandkids. She lived in a four-bedroom house, but she would see her daughter under the bridge before she lost her man.

"You think your boo can take me to get my stuff from Toni's house? I'll give him some gas money," Tori offered.

"That nigga car stays empty, so I'm sure he will. Let me call him," Anna said as she dialed up her male friend's number.

At the sound of gas money, he jumped at the chance and assured her that he was on his way. Anna's kids were at Donna's house playing, so she rode with Tori and helped her to retrieve her items from Toni's house. Toni was serious about Tori getting her stuff because she had everything bagged up and waiting for her by the front door. Anna could see that Toni's door had been replaced and she didn't blame her for putting Tori out. She would have done the same thing if it meant that her and her kids would be safe and out of harm's way. The sisters didn't say anything to each other as Tori grabbed her stuff and threw it in the trunk of the car. Toni was finally able to relax, knowing that Tori and all of her drama was out of her life, hopefully for good.

"Stupid bitch," Tori mumbled once they were back in the car and headed back to the trailer park. Her aunt Donna agreed to let her stay there for a while, but Tori had no intentions of ever sleeping there. She just needed a place to put her clothes, but she would find somewhere else to sleep. Donna's trailer was nice and clean, but Tori hated the environment. She was so deep in her thoughts that she never paid attention to the black Pontiac Grand Am that was following a few cars behind them.

***

"She got all of her stuff out of the house and moved it to some trailer park. I saw the exact one that she went in too," Pluck said to Jaden over the phone.

"That's what's up nigga. Tell your sisters that I need them to get on that ASAP. The money is there, so they don't need to worry about that," Jaden replied.

"I got you big bro, don't worry about nothing," Pluck assured him before he disconnected the call.

Jaden put the phone back in his pocket before he turned his attention back to the wrinkled-faced white sales lady who was helping him.

"Are you done? That was so rude of you," his mother Pam fussed.

"I'm sorry y'all. Yeah, I'm done," he replied.

"Okay good, because this is the one!" Pam yelled excitedly.

"It sure is," Brooklyn and Keller agreed, as they all gazed at the three carat halo diamond engagement ring that the lady was holding up.

"Y'all would pick the most expensive one, huh." He chuckled as he eyed the twenty-thousand-dollar price tag that accompanied it.

"Nigga, I know you're not putting a price tag on my sister," Keller said, hitting him on his arm.

"He damn sure better not be. I wish I could have found one that cost more. She deserves this and more, just for putting up with your crazy ass," Pam argued.

"You got that right," Brooklyn agreed. "Don't try to short change my sister-in-law."

"Never that," Jaden replied. "I don't care what it cost, as long as it makes her happy."

"So, it's a yes to the ring?" the sales lady asked happily with a bright smile on her face.

Her commission check was about to be off the chain with that sell and Jaden knew it. She was being a bitch when they first walked into the store and acted like she didn't want to help them. A younger black lady offered to help, but she snapped on her and made her go help somebody else. She proceeded to show them to the cheapest engagement rings in the case and told them that they could fill out a credit application if they needed to. Jaden was immediately offended, but he held his tongue for the sake of his mother. Although he didn't say anything, he would be damned if he helped to put food on her table with buying anything from her racist ass.

"It's a no for me," Jaden said, wiping the smile right off of her face.

"What! What's wrong with it? It's the perfect ring Jaden," Pam argued.

"I'm buying the ring. I'm just not buying it from her," he replied with a smug look on his face.

"Well, why not?" the sales lady had the nerve to yell. An older gentleman who was standing near the cash registers rushed over to see what was going on.

"Good afternoon everyone. Is there something that I can help you with?" he asked nicely.

"Yep," Jaden replied.

"Okay, I'm the sales manager. What is it that I can do for you?"

"I want to buy that ring, but I don't want her old evil ass to sell it to me. She had an attitude with us from the minute we walked through the door. I want her to help me and get the credit for the sale. If that's going to be a problem, I can take my money and my business elsewhere," Jaden said while pointing to the black sales lady.

"What!" the white sales lady yelled. "I've been helping him for over an hour."

"Correction, you've been following us around for over an hour. We picked out the ring on our own. You tried to show us them cheap ass rings in the other case," Pam interrupted.

"I'm sorry for your trouble sir. You can go now Sophie. I'll get Jackie over here to assist them," the sales manager said, calling the other sales rep over right before he walked away.

Jackie walked over to them with a smile and Pam immediately started telling her what they wanted. Jaden handed his mother his credit card for her to make the purchase while smirking at the frown on Sophie's face.

"The fuck I need a credit app for when I got money. Bye Sophie," Jaden taunted right before she walked away.

"Shut up and watch your mouth boy," Pam scolded her youngest son.

"I'm just saying though ma. She better respect the movement," Jaden said as he pointed to another one of his black lives matter t-shirts that he had on.

"Hush up with that shit Jaden. That's probably why she looked at you sideways in the first place," Pam argued as the other sales lady finalized their purchase.

"Kia is gonna go crazy when she sees that ring." Keller smiled.

"I know she is," Pam agreed. "I got three down and two to go. I just gotta get Caleb and Brian to settle down and get married now. They're the only two that ain't bring me no grandbabies yet."

"Well, you got all that you're gonna get from me," Brooklyn replied.

Jaden didn't say anything, but they all knew that he wanted more kids. Kia wasn't trying to hear him because he messed around too much. She swore to him that they would expand their family once things got better between them, but she never made good on her promise. Jaylynn was almost eleven years old and Kia still took her birth control faithfully. He had to make her trust him again, but he knew that it wasn't going to be easy. Hopefully, the ring that he soon planned to put on her finger would be enough to show her just how serious he really was.

Chapter 15

"Daddy, do you like our hair?" Tigga's daughter, Tia, asked as he drove them home.

"Yeah, I like it, it's pretty," he replied. It was a Sunday, but Keller had taken them to Candace's house earlier that day to get their hair braided. They couldn't seem to stay out of the mirror after that.

"Thank you, daddy. Keller said that she's gonna buy us some more bows to put in it," Tia replied.

"That's good baby," he replied with a smile.

He was happy that his girls didn't feel any differently about Keller after she and their mother fought. After he talked with them that day, they hadn't mentioned anything to him about it again. They still loved Keller the same and he was happy for that.

"Are we stopping at the store daddy?" Talia yelled loudly.

"Yeah, we can stop," Tigga replied.

He usually stopped them at the store before they went home, so her request wasn't unusual. Tigga didn't want to run the risk of running into Terrell, so he went to the store a little further up than the one he usually stopped at. Terrell was known to hang out all over the area, so there really was no telling where he would be. As soon as Tigga stopped in front of the store, he spotted a few regulars hanging around, but his dead beat daddy wasn't one of them. After helping his girls out of the truck, he walked them inside of the store and let them pick out what they wanted. Tigga was about to call Keller to see if she needed anything, before a familiar but unwelcomed voice stopped him in his tracks.

"Are these my pretty little granddaughters?" Terrell said as he walked from the back of the store and stood in front of Tia and Talia.

They looked at him like he was crazy, before running back over to Tigga and grabbing on to his legs. The girls were four and five years old, but they had never seen Terrell a day in their young lives. He was a stranger to them and they treated him as such.

"If you don't get the hell away from my daughters!" Tigga yelled with venom dripping from his voice.

"Y'all don't have to be scared, I'm your grandpa," Terrell said as she completely ignored what Tigga had said.

"You ain't shit to them. This is my last time telling you to keep it pushing. Don't make me knock you the fuck out in this store," Tigga said angrily.

"Knock me out?" Terrell repeated like he was in shock. "Nigga, I'm your daddy and that's how you talk to me. Huh? These are my granddaughters, no matter how you feel about it."

Tigga could see that Terrell was drunk and high out of his mind. He was staggering and his speech was slurred and barely audible. His pupils were dilated and he smelled awful. He was nothing like the man that Tigga knew when he was younger. At one point, Terrell wouldn't be caught dead without a fresh hair cut or nice outfit on. He took pride in his appearance and he taught Tigga to do the same. Terrell was once his hero, but he despised the man that he had become. He was a weak man in his son's eyes. Why else would he allow his addiction to control what he did and when he did it? Why else would he have left his wife and kids on their own to chase after a high that he would never get back again?

"Come on and get y'all stuff so we can go," Tigga said, ignoring his father and walking around him.

His girls followed right behind him, as they got what they wanted and headed up front to the cash register. Terrell stood by the front door with a look of pure jealousy and hate as he watched his son move around the store and ignore him. His granddaughters were absolutely beautiful, but they were scared to death of him. That was Tigga's fault because he never wanted him to be around them.

"Bye, pretty girl." Terrell smiled as he grabbed Tia's hand and held it in his own.

"Daddy," she whined as she snatched her hand away and ran over and stood behind Tigga.

"Nigga, you lost your fucking mind! Don't touch my daughter!" Tigga yelled as he shoved Terrell, making his frail body hit the ground. Regret swept through Tigga's body soon after, but it was too late for him to take it back. He wasn't raised to disrespect his elders, but Terrell always put him in a bad mood whenever he saw him. Tigga just couldn't get over the fact that Terrell abandoned him when he needed him the most. His grandfather was there for him, but it just wasn't the same.

"Come on Tigga. Let it go man," Joe, another known addict in the area said as he approached him. Joe helped Terrell stand to his feet as Tigga grabbed his daughters and headed back to his truck. He hated that his girls had to see him act crazy, but Terrell was always going too far.

"My bad Joe," Tigga said when the older man walked up to his truck.

"You gotta let go of that hate that you have in your heart for him. I know he fucked up with the drugs and everything bruh, but that's still your daddy. He don't deserve that title, but you can't take it away from him," Joe tried to explain.

"I don't hate that nigga Joe; I'm just disappointed in him. He keeps demanding my respect, but what is he doing to earn it? I'll do anything for these two lil girls right here, so I can't respect a man who turns his back on his kids."

"It's the drugs Tigga. That's what has a hold on him. I know what he's going through because I'm fighting the same demons. If you've never been an addict, you wouldn't understand."

"I tried to help that dude Joe. I told my grandmother that I would pay for him to get clean, even though my grandpa begged me not to. I offered to help him get on his feet and get him a place to stay too. When he told my grandmother that he didn't want my help, I stopped trying to offer it. This is the life that he chose to live. He's an addict because he wants to be. I don't want that shit around me or my kids, so I'm done," Tigga said as he started up his truck and pulled off.

His girls didn't seem to care about what had just happened because they were too busy comparing the snacks that they had in their bags. Tigga still made it his business to get Amari a few things because he didn't want her to feel left out. She hadn't been over to his house in a while and he would be lying if he said that he didn't miss her. Amari had become a part of his life, but he had to respect Anaya's wishes to not let her be around him anymore.

"Y'all make sure to give Amari her snacks too," Tigga said when he pulled up in front of Anaya's place and helped them get out.

He shook his head when he saw the 'for rent' sign out front because Anaya still didn't tell him where she was moving to. She was still on her lil girl bullshit, but he didn't have time to play with her. Tigga walked up the steps and rang the doorbell, waiting for Anaya to let the girls in. Although her man lived with her now, Tigga never saw him whenever he went there for his kids. The only reason he knew that he lived there was because his daughters told him. They also told him that Rich was very nice to them, so that made him feel a little better about the situation.

"Mama, look at our braids!" Tia yelled excitedly when Anaya answered the door.

"Keller got her friend to do it this morning," Talia replied, just as happy.

"Who the fuck told her to put that ugly ass shit in my children's head? They don't wear fake hair. That shit is coming out today," Anaya said bitterly.

"Nooooo," Tia cried. "I don't want my braids to come out."

"I don't give a damn what you want. You are too young to be wearing fake hair. Go get the scissors!" Anaya yelled, making Tigga mad.

"Y'all stop crying and go to your room. She not gon' take y'all braids out," Tigga promised them.

"Yes the hell I am!" Anaya yelled, right before he forcefully yanked her outside.

"Bitch, I'm trying with everything in me not to wrap my hands around your fucking neck and choke the life out of you. You can play with my girls if you want to and I'll take your hoe ass back to court and get full custody. You won't be getting a dime in child support then. My daughters better not tell me that you touched a hair on their heads, fake or not. Ole childish, bitter bitch. Fuck with me if you want to," Tigga warned right before he walked off of the porch and got into his truck.

Anaya stood there speechless as her eyes filled with tears. In all the years that she'd known Tigga, she could never recall him speaking to her that way. It was obvious that he was fed up with her and her drama. She was miserable and she hated that he didn't seem to feel the same way. Her life was going downhill and being with Rich wasn't helping. His dumb ass went to jail the day before for driving under the influence and, now, he was begging her to get him out. He knew that their funds were limited and he was causing her to lose even more money. Messing over Tigga for him was the worst mistake that she had ever made and she was now living to regret it.

Chapter 16

Tigga was a little worried, as he used his key and entered his grandparents' home. His grandfather, Bo, had called him earlier, going off about something that Terrell had done. Bo was so upset that Tigga barely understood what he was saying. It had to be really bad because his grandpa was usually calm in any situation. Tigga was out playing basketball at the time, but he promised him that he would be over there as soon as he was done. Tigga couldn't really focus on his game, so he ended up leaving early, just to make sure that everything was okay.

"Bo!" Tigga yelled when he closed and locked the door.

"We're in the den!" Bo yelled back.

Tigga made his way down the long hall and found his grandparents seated in the den, watching the news on their huge screen tv. His grandma was crocheting something just like always, while Bo sat in his recliner. After kissing his grandmother's cheek and shaking hands with his grandfather, Tigga sat down and got comfortable.

"What's up?" he asked, looking to both of them for some answers. Mary kept her head down, focusing on her task, so he turned to look at Bo instead.

"That no good muthafucker stole my wife's money!" Bo fumed as he stood to his feet and started pacing the floor.

"Who stole her money?" Tigga asked.

"That fucking dope fiend son of mine. I swear, that was a waste of perfectly good sperm," Bo fussed.

"Bo!" Mary shrieked. "Don't say that. He's still our only son."

"Fuck that Mary! That nigga ain't no son of mine. And I'm telling you right now that his ass is not allowed in this house no more.

I'm putting a bullet in him if he steps one foot in here and that's a promise."

"What happened? How did he steal her money? Nobody is even telling me anything," Tigga chimed in.

"Terrell got admitted to the hospital and Mary had been going up there to see him. When he called and told her that he was being released, she got him a new outfit and took it up there to him. She must have sat her purse down or wasn't paying attention and his dope fiend ass stole all of her money. Almost two hundred dollars and he took it all," Bo yelled.

"What!" Tigga yelled as he, too, stood to his feet.

"My wife makes sure he has a hot meal and a shower damn near every day and that's how he repaid her. By stealing her fucking money," Bo continued to fuss.

"I'm going see his ass," Tigga replied angrily.

"Tyler no, don't even worry about it. I just have to be more careful when he's around," Mary said, making her husband even angrier.

"He ain't gon' be around. I just told you that I don't want that crack head in my house and I don't want you nowhere around his ass. We've done too much for that boy for him to do that to you. I went through this shit enough and I ain't going through it no more," Bo barked.

"What do you want me to do? That's my son," Mary cried.

Tigga felt so bad, seeing his grandmother shed tears over Terrell's punk ass yet again. This wasn't the first time that his father stole from his grandparents, but it had been a while since he did. He started out stealing from the company by writing checks to himself, but Bo quickly caught on to that scheme. When that no longer worked, Terrell used to convince Mary to give him money for different things, but Bo put a stop to that too. When his addiction really started to spiral out of control, nothing of value was safe around him. He would steal electronics and everything else that he could sell to make a quick dollar. Mary's purse had often been the target of his addiction and it seemed as if nothing had changed.

"I know you love him baby, but Terrell needs help. Until he gets it, I can't allow him to keep hurting you like this," Bo said while hugging and trying to comfort his wife.

"He don't want no help grandma. You know I tried to help him several times and he always turned me down. Terrell is a grown man. He's not your responsibility anymore," Tigga pointed out.

"I know baby, but that's still your father. You have to answer to God for how you treat him. He told me about how you pushed him down not too long ago," Mary informed him.

"Good for his ass," Bo mumbled.

"Bo!" Mary scolded. "Don't encourage his behavior. And don't you go trying to confront him Tyler. Just leave it alone. Y'all are right; I have to let Terrell be."

"I'm not gonna do him nothing. I just want to talk to him about what he did," Tigga replied.

"No Tyler, just let it go. I don't need nothing else to be worried about," his grandmother begged.

He nodded his head, but he had no intentions of honoring her request. Terrell was going too far and he seemed to not care about who he hurt in the process. Tigga sat down and waited until his grandmother had calmed down. Once she left to go start her dinner, he hung around and talked to his grandpa for a while.

"Go see that nigga. And if he say some slick shit out his mouth, knock him right back on his ass," Bo said seriously.

"Say no more," Tigga replied as he stood up and walked out of the house.

***

Terrell stood outside of the store, pacing up and down the sidewalk. His anxiety was through the roof and he needed to get high like never before. After being admitted to the hospital for an entire week, he was long overdue for something to smoke. Terrell had started feeling bad a few weeks prior and his mother begged him to let her take him to the emergency room. He declined, but he regretted that decision soon after. Joe ended up having to call an ambulance for him when he passed out in front of one of their store front hangouts. He could hardly breathe, due to the respiratory infection that he had developed. The doctors said that it was a result of his drug use, but he wasn't trying to hear that. They tried to admit him into a treatment facility, but they couldn't force him to stay. He had some money in his pockets, so he called up one of his suppliers and begged him to bring him something to smoke.

"Bout damn time," Terrell blurted when he saw who he had been waiting for.

His mouth started watering, just thinking about what was in store. Terrell had lifted almost two hundred dollars from his mother's purse earlier that day at the hospital, so he had enough for a decent meal and some liquor too. He knew that she would be upset about him stealing from her, but she would forgive him just like she always did.

"What the business is?" Leo asked, as he walked up on Terrell.

Leo had been laying low for a while since he was a wanted man, but money still needed to be made. Terrell and some of the other men in the area were some of his best customers, so he came whenever they called.

"I got one hundred to spend. Hook me up Leo," Terrell begged desperately.

"Nigga, where did you get one hundred dollars from. Who did you rob or steal from to get that much cash?" Leo questioned. Terrell had never spent more than twenty dollars at a time, so he was shocked to hear that he had that much money.

"Don't worry about that. You trying to get it or not?" Terrell asked impatiently.

"Fuck you talking to like that nigga? You must not know how I get down. I'll knock your junkie ass out and take your money from you," Leo threatened.

"Come on man. Don't do me like that. It's been a while and I'm in need," Terrell pleaded.

"Nah nigga, now you gon' wait on me. You might be ready to act right by the time I come out of the store," Leo said as he walked away cockily.

Terrell watched him walk away and kicked himself for getting out of pocket. He was so anxious to smoke something that his attitude wasn't the best lately. He waited for a few more minutes, until he saw Leo walk back out and towards where he was standing.

"My bad man. I'm out here losing my damn mind," Terrell said apologetically. He got excited when he saw Leo bend down to retrieve the product from his sock. That excitement didn't last long because something else had grabbed the youngster's attention soon after. When a bronze colored Lexus truck pulled up, Leo's focus stayed on it the entire time until it came to a stop.

"It must be my lucky day." Leo smiled as he walked towards the truck with Terrell hot on his trail.

"Who is that?" Terrell questioned.

"That's my bitch. You gotta wait to get serviced now," Leo said, waiting to see if Keller was going to exit the truck.

The dark tint didn't allow him to see inside, but he was sure that it was her. He could spot that truck from a mile away, especially since he use to always follow her around. Leo knew that he had done Keller dirty the last time he saw her and he was desperate to make things right with her again. He couldn't accept the fact that Keller had replaced him and moved on with another man. They had too much history for her to just walk away from him like that. Leo watched the truck intensely until the door swung open. His smile immediately faded when he saw Keller's man getting out of the truck instead of her.

"Shit," Terrell mumbled when he saw Tigga walking over towards them.

He was sure that his mother had told him about what happened, but he wasn't in the mood to deal with his son at the moment. He was going through some serious withdrawals and getting crack was the only thing on his mind. Tigga was a man on a mission. He originally went there to confront Terrell, but his luck got even better when he saw Leo standing there with him. He clearly remembered his face from the few pictures that Jaden had showed him. Tigga's anger reached a new level when he thought about the bruises on Keller's neck after Leo choked her out in the mall. He put his thoughts of Terrell and everything else on the back burner as he ran up to Leo and swung on him. Leo was caught off guard by his much bigger opponent, but he refused to go down. He swung back with the speed of lightning and caught Tigga in his jaw. The love lick seemed to infuriate Tigga and he grew angrier. Leo was paper thin compared to him, so he used that to his advantage. He used one of his big arms to pin him up against the wall, while he continued to pummel his face with his free hand. The punches to his face felt like fire to Leo and he now knew how Keller felt all the times he'd hit her.

"Swing on me how you used to swing on my girl bitch!" Tigga growled as he continued to reign blows to Leo's face and body. He decided to let him go so that he could fight back, but it was no use. He had worked Leo's little body over and he fell to the ground as soon as he did.

"Ahh! Fuck!" Leo moaned in agony when Tigga's foot came crashing down on his back and side. It felt like something had broken inside of him and the pain he was in was almost unbearable.

"Calm down man, that's enough," Terrell said as he tried to pull Tigga away from Leo's battered body. That was a huge mistake and he found that out the minute he laid a figure on his son. Without thinking twice about it, Tigga's closed fist came crashing down on Terrell's face, causing him to fall to the ground right next to Leo. A few other people were watching what went down, but they all knew to mind their own business. Terrell just had to be the one to intervene.

"The fuck wrong with you putting your hands on me, nigga. And where my grandma's money at punk?" Tigga fumed as he went through all of Terrell's pockets. Once he located a bunch of twenties in one of Terrell's pockets, he pulled it out and stuck in his own.

"Man wait, don't take my money," Terrell begged as he stood to his feet and tried to walk after his son. That was his only way to get something to smoke and Tigga was trying to take it.

"Fuck out of here. That's my grandma's money nigga. You ain't getting high off of her shit today," Tigga spat right before he got in the truck and sped away. He called his grandpa to let him know that he would be bringing his grandma's money back to her shortly.

"Fuck!" Terrell yelled as he kicked a glass beer bottle and watched it shatter into pieces. He was already going crazy waiting on Leo to show up. He was really about to lose his mind now, since he couldn't even afford to buy anything. He watched as Leo slowly stood to his feet and propped himself up against the concrete store wall. Although he was badly beaten and bloodied, Terrell needed his help. He needed to smoke something bad and he wondered if Leo would give him credit until he found a way to get a few dollars. Usually, he would wash cars or do a little handiwork for people in the area to keep money in his pockets. That didn't always happen and he couldn't wait any longer to get high.

"On my mama, that nigga is dead," Leo swore as he spit a wad of blood from his mouth.

"How do you even know him?" Terrell questioned.

"Nah nigga, how the fuck do you know him? Who is his grandma whose money you stole?" Leo asked.

"His grandma is my mama. That's my son," Terrell revealed.

"Your son? The fuck did you have kids?" Leo inquired.

"I got two kids, nigga. I had a wife at one time too. I ain't been a junkie all my life. That nigga hates me though. He turned my daughter Tessa against me too."

"Tessa? What Tessa?" Leo asked as he described Tessa to her father.

"Yeah, that's her," Terrell nodded.

"So, that nigga is Tessa's brother?"

"Yep, that's my son Tigga." Terrell nodded once again.

"That bitch been playing me for a while now," Leo said angrily as he thought about Keller. She was always telling him that she was out with Tessa or at Tessa's house and now he knew why. She had been fucking Tessa's brother all along and making him look like a damn fool.

"Huh?" Terrell asked in confusion.

"Where that nigga live at? I already know the area, but I mean the exact house that he lives in? And don't try to say you don't know either," Leo warned.

"Man, I really don't know. I just told you that the nigga hates me. I don't know shit about where he and Tessa lay their heads. The only time I see him is on the streets or at my mama and daddy's house," Terrell replied.

"Where that's at?" Leo inquired.

"Nah man, I ain't involving my mama and daddy in this mess. If I knew where Tigga lived at, I swear I would tell you. That nigga disrespected me for the last time. I don't give a damn about what happens to him, but I can't let nothing happen to my parents."

"Nothing is gonna happen to your people, man. If your son be over there like you say, maybe I can follow him and catch his ass slippin'. With or without your help, I'm gon' find the nigga," Leo promised.

"Well, its gon' have to be without my help," Terrell replied as he attempted to walk away.

"So, you not trying to smoke nothing?" Leo said, stopping him from going any further. Terrell turned around and salivated at the sight before him. Leo had a small plastic bag filled to the rim with crack. He dangled it in front of Terrell's face and the decision was already made. Terrell would have sold his soul to the devil for some dope and Leo already knew that.

"Let me get something on credit Leo," Terrell begged while never taking his eyes off of the product.

"Nigga, I'm willing to give something for free if you tell me what I need to know," Leo offered. He saw that Terrell wanted to give in, but he was still battling with himself about what to do. Leo wasn't taking no for an answer, so he decided to sweeten the pot just a little.

"Look here, I know your punk ass son took all your money, but I'm still willing to give you one hundred dollars' worth of product at no cost. Just give me the address. Your people will be safe; you have my word," Leo promised. He saw Terrell breaking down right before his eyes, causing a huge smile to appear on his face.

"Alright," Terrell agreed as he watched Leo take some of the dope out of the bag.

He gave him his parents' address and even described the house to him, color and all. His need for drugs was greater than anything else, including his family's safety. Once Leo put the drugs in his hands, Terrell almost ran to the back of the store to get his mind right. Leo got back into his car and drove towards his brother's apartment. He was moving at a snail's pace, as a result of the beating that Tigga had just put on him. Although he would definitely be getting at him soon, it wasn't about to be that night. He was in too much pain to do anything but drive home and take a hot shower. Thankfully, his brother was a pill popper because he needed something strong to get rid of the pain that he was in. Leo was heated, but Tigga wasn't the only one that had him angry. Keller had played him for a fool and she had to get dealt with too. He couldn't believe that her sneaky ass had the nerve to cheat on him after she always accused him of doing her wrong. It was true that he did his dirt too, but Keller played the innocent role well. Leo always accused her of messing around, but he never thought that she actually did it. He only did that to throw her off when he was doing his dirt. She swore that she didn't start messing with her new man until after they broke up, but that was a lie. The fact that the nigga was Tessa's brother spoke volumes as far as he was concerned. Leo couldn't even lie; his heart was broken and he was hurt. It was cool though. He was determined to make Keller and her man feel the same kind of pain that he was feeling and more.

Chapter 17

"Nigga, I wish I was there to see you beat his hoe ass down." Jaden laughed as he and Tigga sipped their beers and talked.

Tigga was filling him in on everything that happened with him and Leo a few days prior, and he was all into the conversation. Tigga looked like a clean cut, innocent type of person, but he had a mean alter ego that Jaden loved to see come out. He had some lethal hands and that was proven when they had a fight with some dudes when they went out to the club one night. One of the dudes tried to talk crazy to Tigga about something and he ended up getting carried out of the club after Tigga knocked his stupid ass out. That was the first time Jaden saw Tigga's crazy side, but he had mad respect for him after that.

"Fuck that dude. Ole pussy ass can't even fight, but want put his hands on females. Keller probably could have beat him if she wasn't so scared of the nigga," Tigga replied.

"That nigga had her scared to death too. I don't know what the fuck he used to tell her like that," Jaden said, shaking his head.

"It's all good though. She don't have to worry about a nigga putting his hands on her no more. I'll leave her alone before I hit her," Tigga said honestly.

"I feel you, bruh. But what was your pops doing talking to Leo? I wonder where he know him from," Jaden questioned.

"Nigga probably was buying some dope or something. I don't know and I really don't care." Tigga shrugged.

"Man, this bitch better come on. I'm ready to bring my ass back home," Jaden fussed as he checked the time on his phone.

He and Tigga were back at the strip club, waiting on Bianca.

She called and told Jaden that she had all of his money and he was there to collect it. Jaden was waiting for his supplier to get some more product, so he didn't have anything else for her to sell at the moment. He didn't want to be out by himself, so he got Tigga to meet him there to have a few drinks.

"Did you tell her that you were here?" Tigga questioned.

"Nah, but I told her that I was coming through around eight," Jaden replied as he scrolled down his contact list and found Bianca's number. He had it stored under 'Work' because that's all that there was between them now. He sent her a text asking when she was coming out and waited for her to reply.

"So, when are you popping the question? Keller told me that they broke you in the jewelry store." Tigga chuckled.

"They did, but it's all good. My baby is worth it. I want to plan something special and do it then," Jaden replied right as Bianca responded to his text. His face immediately twisted up into a frown, making Tigga wonder what was going on.

"What's up? What you frowning for?" Tigga asked him.

"This stupid bitch ain't even here. She talking bout she thought I knew that she was off tonight. How the fuck did she expect me to know that? I wouldn't have even came over here if I knew that," Jaden fumed.

"Damn," Tigga sighed. "Well, go handle your business and go on back home. I'm going lay-up with Keller and watch some tv or some shit."

"I wasted my fucking time even coming here," Jaden continued to fuss as he followed Tigga out to the parking lot.

"Keep your dick in your pants, nigga. Call me if that gets to be too hard to do," Tigga said, right before he gave him dap and got into his car.

Jaden laughed at his remark, right before he got into his own car and pulled away from the building. He usually wouldn't be worried about getting his money from Bianca, but she had been holding on to it for almost a month now. She had a little over five grand for him and that was the money that he wanted to use to take Kia and Jaylynn shopping for the weekend. Once Jaden pulled up to her complex and parked, he hopped out of his car and banged on her door. When Bianca opened the door wearing nothing but a lace bra and matching thongs, Jaden knew it was about to be some shit.

"Come in and let me get your money," Bianca said as she turned and sauntered off to the back of her house.

"Lord, have mercy. I need to get the fuck up out of here," Jaden mumbled to himself as he stood right by the front door. He didn't know if Tigga was joking or not, but he was about to take him up on his offer and give him a call. He needed a distraction to keep from doing something that he knew he would regret later on. He had been doing right by Kia and he wanted to keep it that way. As soon as Jaden pulled his phone from his pocket to call Tigga, Bianca came walking back into the room holding a gold envelope.

"It's all there, but you can count it if you want to," Bianca told him.

"I don't need to count it. I know how to find you if anything is missing," Jaden replied.

"Did you bring me some more to sell? I don't have anything left and people have been asking."

"I'm all out for now. I should be getting something soon though. I'll call you when it comes through," he replied while reaching for the envelope.

"Why is that the only time that you call me? I don't hear from you anymore unless it's about business," Bianca said, moving the envelope away from his outstretched hand.

"The fuck you mean? We don't have shit else to talk about. I'm about to be a married man. I ain't on that cheating shit no more," Jaden replied while snatching the envelope from her hand.

"You're about to be, but you're not married yet," Bianca said as she dropped down to her knees and looked up at him. She licked her full, pouty lips right before pulling down Jaden's sweat pants and boxers.

"Girl, chill out," Jaden protested weakly as she pulled out his stiff erection.

The sight of Bianca on her knees twirling her tongue around the head of his dick just did something to him. Jaden hissed when she finally stopped teasing and took him into her mouth. He grabbed the back of her head and thrust his pelvis forward, encouraging her to take a little more. Bianca gagged a little, but that didn't stop her from trying to please him. She was moaning and humming like she was receiving pleasure, instead of being the one to give it. The vibration from her mouth, coupled with the noises she was making, had Jaden ready to explode. He was in the zone and remaining faithful to Kia was the furthest thing from his mind. He came out of his lustful daze soon after, when his phone started ringing to the Wifey ringtone.

"Ugh," Bianca mumbled as Jaden pushed her away from him. He quickly pulled his boxers and pants up before grabbing the phone and looking down at her. She knew what he was about to say, so she said it before he could even open his mouth.

"I already know, be quiet," Bianca sassed while rolling her eyes to the sky.

"Hey baby," Jaden said when he answered Kia's call.

"I'm hungry," Kia whined into the phone.

"What you wanna eat? I'll pick something up for you right quick," Jaden replied.

"I don't know. Come get me and we can ride around and see what's open," Kia suggested.

"I'm on my way," Jaden promised.

"Okay, call me when you're outside," Kia said before they disconnected.

"I'm out," Jaden said to Bianca once he made sure the phone was hung up.

"Really Jaden? She calls and says that she's hungry and it's forget Bianca, huh?"

"The fuck you thought. You already know what it is," he replied while unlocking her front door to leave.

"Fuck you, Jaden!" Bianca yelled as tears came to her eyes.

"Nah, I'm straight. Shit wasn't all that good anyway. It's all business from now on, so I won't even be meeting you at your house no more. I'll hit you up when shit is sweet again," he replied as he walked out of her front door and got into his car.

Bianca was pissed, but he didn't give a damn. She slammed her front door behind him, but she could kiss his ass for all he cared. She already knew what the deal was when it came to Kia. He didn't give a damn if his woman wanted a glass of water. Everything was shut down until she got it, no questions asked. Bianca was no better than Tori. She caught feelings and got mad because he didn't return them. And just like he did with Tori, he was cutting off all personal interactions with her too. He just prayed that Bianca didn't take things as far as Tori did. If so, he wouldn't have a problem dealing with her just the same. His people still hadn't dealt with Tori yet, but her time was coming sooner than she thought. She was gonna get comfortable and stop hiding eventually.

Chapter 18

Jaden rubbed his throbbing temples as he drove away from the movie theater. Not only did he have to deal with Jaylynn's loud, constant talking, but he had his two nieces staying the night over too. Bryce and Taylor wanted to do a date night, so he and Kia agreed to keep their girls. Their baby boy was with Co-Co and Dwight, so they had the entire day and night to themselves. He and Kia took them to the Riverwalk to shop before going out to eat and to the movies. He definitely needed a strong drink after all of that. They had him second guessing having more kids after spending the entire day with them. After Jaden stopped at the store for snacks, they were pulling up to their house about thirty minutes later. It was after nine at night and everybody was drained.

"You okay boo?" Kia said, laughing at him. Jaylynn and her cousins were a couple of characters and they kept her very well entertained. Jaden was only used to being with his daughter, so they were driving him crazy with all the questions they kept asking him.

"Hell no, I ain't alright. I never knew they talked so damn much when they got together. They got me with a headache," he complained.

"I'm going to go make sure they take a bath and get in the bed. You want me to fix you a drink?" Kia offered.

"Yeah and make it strong," Jaden replied as he threw his tired body across their bed.

He pulled out his phone and read the text messages that Pluck had sent him earlier. Although he had followed Tori to the trailer park, he hadn't seen her show up there since that very first time. It wasn't like he was there day and night, so there was no telling what time Tori was coming and going. Jaden was ready for her to get dealt with, but he couldn't do anything until she came out of hiding. Pluck's sisters had already been paid and they were ready to show Jaden that the money was well worth it. Jaden was tired, but he didn't realize that he'd fallen asleep until Kia shook his leg a while later. She smelled just like her pink Dove soap, so he knew that she had just taken a shower. Her hair was tied up and she had on a pink night shirt, but she was still the prettiest girl that Jaden had ever seen, aside from his daughter.

"What happened to my drink?" he asked while rubbing the sleep from his eyes.

"I came in here to ask you what you wanted, but you were knocked out," Kia replied.

"I'm tired as hell, but I still want something to drink. Patron is cool."

"Okay, go take your shower and I'll have something waiting for you when you get out," Kia said as she turned down the covers on their bed.

"And have this off when I come out too," he said, tugging at her nightshirt.

"Okay." Kia blushed and smiled.

She turned on their flat screen tv and found a movie to watch, right as the shower water started to run. After taking out a pair of boxers and a t-shirt for Jaden, she went into the kitchen to fix his drink. Once that was done, she checked on Jaylynn and her guests before going back to her bedroom and locking the door. Kia had just gotten comfortable on her side of the bed when Jaden's phone started ringing. Kia picked it up, but she sat it right back down when 'Work' popped up on the screen. She didn't know if it was the legal or illegal business that was calling and she really didn't care. She couldn't help whoever was calling either way. Kia got comfortable again, but a text message was coming through soon after. She grabbed the phone again and tears immediately came to her eyes when she started reading.

Since you won't answer the phone I'll just say what I have to say via text message. I tried, but I can't have a no strings attached sexual relationship with anyone and that includes you. I'm a very emotional person and I get attached once I become intimate with someone. I've allowed you to use my body and make a fool of me for months, but I can't, no, I won't, do it anymore. With that being said, don't worry about bringing me anything else to sell. You've already cut off our personal relationship but, for my sanity, I need to cut off our business relationship as well. I'll dance until the day I receive my degree before I keep degrading myself for you. I wish you all the best, but I love me too much to keep being your fool.

Peace, Bianca

Kia shook her head in disgust and wiped the tears from her eyes. She had never tried to fool herself into thinking that Jaden was a saint, but she was really fed up with it. He always claimed that he only let women work for him because it was easier, but that was a bunch of bullshit. He fucked every female that he came in contact with and that was his reason for always keeping them around. Kia got out of the bed and grabbed a pair of jeans and a t-shirt from her drawer, right as the shower stopped running. She needed some air or she was bound to kill Jaden the moment he opened his mouth to lie to her.

"What the hell you got dressed for?" Jaden frowned when he walked back into the bedroom with nothing but a towel wrapped around his waist.

"I'm getting the fuck out of here before I kill your dog ass," Kia said as she grabbed her flip flops from the closet and pulled the scarf from her head.

"Kill me for what? The fuck did I do now?" Jaden asked, while dropping the towel and pulling his boxers on.

"This is what you did. The same thing your dog ass always do. Lying, cheating mutherfucker!" Kia yelled while shoving the phone in his hands.

She had the text message already pulled up and waiting for him to see. She knew that the excuses and lies were coming, so she just stood there and waited.

"Man," Jaden sighed as he ran his hand down his face. "It ain't even like that."

"I'm so done Jaden. I swear I am. I love you so fucking much that I don't love myself enough. Crazy as it sounds, I feel just what her text message was saying. I'm degrading myself by letting you do the shit that you do. I'll go crazy if I don't get away from you. I can't take this no more," Kia cried as she grabbed her purse and tried to leave.

"Baby, I swear I don't fuck with that girl like that. I fucked up once before, but that shit is dead and over with. She even said so in her message," Jaden said as he blocked the door to keep her from leaving.

"It still happened though Jaden! You cannot be faithful and you've proven that over and over again. Just let me go and you can do whatever you want to do with no worries."

"I can't let you go Kia. I know I messed up a lot in the past baby, but I'm done. I swear on my life that I'm done," Jaden said with tears building up in his eyes.

"That makes two of us. Get out of my way," Kia said as she wiped her eyes with the sleeves of her shirt.

Jaden saw the look in her eyes and he knew that she meant every word. She was tired of him and she'd finally reached her breaking point. His heart felt like it was beating out of his chest as he watched the love of his life try to walk out on him. As much as she probably needed to leave, he just couldn't let her. The risk of her never coming back was too much for him to bear.

"No Kia," Jaden said, just above a whisper as he lowered his head.

"No? No, what?" Kia asked with her hand on her hip.

"I can't let you leave," he replied while looking her directly in her eyes.

"You really don't have a choice. Move out of my way before I get my Taser and zap your dog ass," Kia threatened.

"Did you forget that Jaylynn has company over here?" Jaden questioned.

"I don't give a damn. That's your nieces. Call Bryce and tell him to come and get them if you can't handle it. Jaylynn can stay right here with you."

"And where are you trying to go?" he asked her.

"Anywhere but here," Kia replied.

"No, baby please, just go to sleep and we can talk about it in the morning," Jaden begged.

"There's nothing to talk about Jaden. I need to get away from you and I'm not waiting until morning."

"I'll go sleep on the sofa," Jaden offered, trying anything to get her to stay. He could have slept in the spare bedroom, but he didn't want Kia trying to leave while he was sleeping.

"Not good enough. We'll still be under the same roof," Kia snapped.

"You know what? Fuck it! I'm trying to make this shit right, but fuck it. Ain't nobody leaving up out of this bitch. I'm locking this shit down!" Jaden fumed as he stormed off to the front of the house and grabbed the keys that they kept dangling in the lock.

"So, you do wrong and we get locked down," Kia said as she stood there and watched him pace the floor.

"I'm trying to make the shit right, but you won't let me. You didn't even let me explain myself," Jaden said as he continued to march back and forth, like his nerves were bad.

"Did you fuck her?" Kia asked, causing him to stop and look at her. When Jaden lowered his head without replying, she already had her answer. "That's what I thought. Ain't nothing to explain."

"The shit wasn't even that deep like you're trying to make it seem."

"I don't give a damn how deep it was. So, it's cool if I go out and fuck another nigga, just as long as it's not that deep?" Kia asked.

"You trying to die for some dick?" Jaden questioned angrily.

"If that was the case, your ass would have been dead. All the pussy you be running up in," Kia snapped as she walked back to her bedroom and slammed the door. As soon a she got out of her clothes, she grabbed her phone to call her mother.

"Hey my love," Mo said cheerily when she answered the phone.

"I need you, Mo," Kia cried into the phone. "I'm so tired of this shit."

Mo took a deep breath and tried her best to control her anger. She hated to hear her babies crying for any reason, no matter how grown they were.

"I'm listening Kia. Talk to me and don't you leave a damn thing out," Mo warned her.

And talk was exactly what Kia did. She poured her heart out on the phone with her mother and she didn't leave out any details. Mo listened to her cry and rant for hours, but she never interrupted her. She was never the judgmental type, so she didn't criticize her daughter for what she had put up with over the years. Kia didn't call to ask for her opinion and she didn't try to offer it. After lifting a huge burden from her shoulders, Kia fell asleep with a calmness that she hadn't felt in a while. Talking to Mo proved to be exactly what she needed and she was happy that she made the call.

A few hours into her deep slumber, Kia was awakened by a dip in the center of her bed. She didn't even have to open her eyes to know that it was Jaden coming to get in the bed with her. The time on her cable box let her know that it was almost five in the morning and the sun would be rising soon. Kia's first mind told her to get up and go to the guest bedroom, but Jaden wrapped his arm around her and pulled her close to him before she could make a move.

"Please don't leave me, baby. I'm so sorry," Jaden said as he buried his face in the back of her neck. Kia's entire body stiffened when she felt the warm tears that he was shedding fall on the back of her nightshirt.

Chapter 19

Over three weeks had passed since Jaden and Kia's big blowup and nothing had changed between them since then. Kia was still giving Jaden the silent treatment and he was losing his mind. She had never ignored him for that long and he couldn't take it. He tried everything in his power to make things right with her, but she wasn't trying to hear it. Jaden cried, begged, and pleaded for her forgiveness, but Kia was still being stubborn. He even changed his cellphone number to show her how serious he was, but nothing was working. It was a waste of his time to even lock the house down. Kia worked from home now, so she wasn't fazed. Jaden was so scared that she was going to leave him while he was at work that he missed an entire week, just to stay home and watch her. Once he was confident that she wasn't going anywhere, he returned to his normal schedule at the shop. After doing everything that he thought would work, Jaden finally decided on the perfect plan. He wanted to wait to do something special before he proposed to Kia, but he needed her to know just how serious he was about them being together. He couldn't picture his life without her in it and she needed to know that.

"You nervous bro?" Tigga asked as he and Jaden sat in Dominic's backyard, smoking and drinking beers.

Jaden had gone over there to drop Jaylynn off and pick up the food that Brooklyn was preparing for him. He had planned an intimate dinner at home for him and Kia, then he was going to pop the question. Brooklyn had gotten him some rose petals and scented candles to help set the atmosphere. Kia was out shopping with Keller, so he would have enough time to get everything together.

"Nah man. This shit is long overdue," Jaden replied honestly.

"This nigga is about to be a married man. It's about damn time," Dominic said, giving him dap.

"Kia ain't putting up with my shit no more man. I'm all out of chances, so it's time for me to get it right. Crazy thing is, I was already trying to get my shit together. Aside from that last slip up with Bianca, I've been doing good," Jaden replied.

"You can't be married and talking about having slip ups though bruh," Dominic preached.

"Nigga, what?" Jaden said, waving him off. "You, of all people, can't tell me shit."

"Why? What he do wrong?" Tigga questioned.

"This nigga made a baby with Brooklyn while he was engaged to another woman. Then, he got married to the other woman and made another baby with Brooklyn after that. You think I'm listening to anything that he have to say?" Jaden questioned while pointing to his brother-in-law.

"You should be trying to listen so you don't make the same mistakes I made. My shit is sweet now though nigga. Me and my wife are good," Dominic replied.

"After all the bullshit that y'all went through, y'all can't help but be good. Y'all shit was dysfunctional for a long ass time too. Now, you want to act like a therapist or some shit, since you and Brooklyn finally got it together," Jaden fussed.

"Fuck you, boy. I see your ole love sick ass always coming to me for advice though, huh. I must be doing something right," Dominic challenged.

"I can't even front bro; I want something like what you and my sister have. I just want to be happy with one woman for the rest of my life. The shit can't be that hard."

"It's not hard at all if that's what you really want." Dominic shrugged.

Jaden nodded his head in agreement. Being with Kia for the rest of his life was indeed what he wanted to do and there was no doubt about it. She deserved the world and everything it in, and he was determined to give it to her.

"Okay Jaden, everything is still hot, so you shouldn't have to warm it. You can turn your oven on low and just put the pans inside to stay warm if y'all don't plan on eating it right away," Brooklyn said when she came out of the house with two insulated bags with pans of food in both.

"Good looking out sis," he said as he and Tigga stood and took the bags from her hands.

"Co-Co said to save him some because he know that y'all are not going to eat it all," Brooklyn said, relaying her cousin's message. Brooklyn had made stuffed shrimp, crab cakes, pasta, and blackened fish for Jaden and Kia to enjoy. She also made enough for her family, but she never did tell that to her cousin. David and Candace were on their way over for dinner and Co-Co would die if he knew that.

"Forget Co-Co. I'll sell his ass a plate," Jaden said, making his sister laugh before she walked away.

"Aye bruh, tell that nigga David that he been acting shady with us too. That nigga be acting like he can't even come outside no more," Tigga said as Dominic walked them to the car.

"That boy is a family man now. Him and his wife are about to come over here in a few," Dominic replied.

"He was another one with a dysfunctional ass relationship. That nigga was getting pussy in the work place," Jaden said as he fell out laughing. He proceeded to tell Tigga about David's sexual relationship with Dwight's cousin, Yasmine, making him laugh right along with him.

"Don't laugh with that clown. He got him a lil taste of her too," Dominic informed Tigga.

"Where she at now?" Tigga asked, referring to the woman in question.

"Dead," Jaden replied. "She hopped on the wrong dick and got sent to meet her maker."

"Damn," Tigga said as he shook his head solemnly.

He and Jaden loaded the food up in Jaden's black Challenger and went on their way. Jaden had picked Tigga up from his house, so she had to drop him off before he went to his own house. Tigga sent Keller a text to see how long she was going to be because he was ready to lay up with her for the rest of the day.

"Alright my nigga, hit me up if you need me. Congrats bruh," Tigga said as he gave Jaden dap and got out of his car.

"I appreciate that man, but you probably won't hear from me until tomorrow or the day after," Jaden replied, right before he pulled off.

He was a nervous wreck as he drove home, occasionally looking at the ring that would soon adorn Kia's finger. There was no doubt in Jaden's mind that Kia would accept his proposal, but he knew that he still had to work hard to earn her trust back. After walking into their house, Jaden put the oven on warm and put the pans that Brooklyn had given him inside. The food smelled good already and he hadn't even uncovered them yet. Kia loved strawberry cheesecake, so Jaden had gotten a fresh one from the bakery earlier that day, along with a bottle of her favorite wine. Jaden planned to do everything in the dining room, so he sprinkled the rose petals all over the table and floor and placed the unlit candles all around the room. Once everything was done to his liking, Jaden snapped a picture and sent it to his sister. He needed to make sure that he had done everything just like she told him to. Once Brooklyn sent back the thumbs up emoji, Jaden smiled and prepared to go take his shower. When he opened the door to their bedroom, something seemed off, but he couldn't put his finger on it. The dresser that was once full of Kia's perfume seemed a little less cluttered. Jaden shrugged it off and proceeded to get undressed to clean himself up. When he pulled the closet door open, Jaden stopped in his tracks as his breath got caught up in his throat.

"What the fuck! Come on man, no!" Jaden yelled as he stepped into their almost empty walk-in closet. Everything that once belonged to Kia was gone, leaving only his clothes and shoes visible. He ran out of the closet and proceeded to open the now empty drawers that her lingerie and pajamas used to be in.

"Baby, please don't do this to me." Jaden panicked as his heart damn near beat out of his chest. He grabbed his phone and dialed Kia's number, right as he ran into Jaylynn's bedroom to see if any of her items were missing. Jaden's face was masked in confusion when he saw that his daughter's closet was still practically full. He could see that some of the items had been removed, but over half of everything remained intact. The same went with her drawers. Some of them were empty, while others were filled to maximum capacity. When Kia's phone went to voicemail for the third time, Jaden dialed Keller's number, since the two of them were together.

"What's up Jaden?" Keller asked when she answered the phone.

"Keller, please tell me that Kia is with you," Jaden hurriedly spoke into the phone.

"What? No, I'm with Tessa and Co-Co in the mall. What's wrong?" Keller asked him.

"Man, I don't know what the fuck is going on. She told me that she was going shopping with you but, when I came home, all of her stuff was gone."

"She was supposed to come with me, but she called and said that she changed her mind. Did y'all get into it again?" Keller asked.

"No, not since the last time. I thought shit was getting a little better since she was starting to talk to me again. I don't know what the hell is going on with her now."

"Did you try calling her phone?" Kia questioned.

"Yeah, but she didn't answer. Try to call her on three-way for me Keller," Jaden begged.

"Okay, hold on and don't say nothing," Keller told him.

"I won't," Jaden said right before she made the call. The phone was silent for a while, but Kia's voice caught his attention soon after when she answered the phone.

"Where the hell are you?" Keller yelled as soon as her sister picked up.

"I'm at home," Kia replied.

"Your ass not at home. I'm here and you ain't nowhere to be found!" Jaden yelled, even though Keller told him to shut up.

"Let me rephrase that. I'm at my own house," Kia replied.

"Your own house?" Jaden repeated. "What kind of fucking games are you playing Kia?"

"That's your problem now. You think everything is a game, but I'm tired of playing with you, Jaden. What, you thought it was all good because I hung around for a few weeks? I was just waiting for my move-in date to roll around nigga. I told you that I was done and I meant that shit. And don't worry, we'll share custody of Jaylynn. That's why I left half of her stuff there with you," Kia replied.

"I can't believe that you didn't even tell me anything," Keller fussed at her sister.

"You tell Tigga too much and I didn't need him running his mouth to my ex," Kia said, putting emphasis on the word 'ex'.

"The fuck you mean your ex? You better be far out of the state of Louisiana, playing these stupid ass games with me Kia!" Jaden yelled angrily.

"I'll call you later with my new number Keller. This one is about to get changed," Kia said before she disconnected their call.

"Oh my God. I can't believe this," Keller said in shock, as Co-Co and Tessa bombarded her with a million questions. Jaden had already hung up the phone when she started telling the both of them what had just happened.

"I can't believe she really left him," Tessa said as they walked back to Keller's truck.

"I need to go over there and make sure that Jaden is okay. I've been around him damn near my entire life. It's gonna be weird with him and Kia not being together," Keller said sadly.

"I told him that Kia was getting tired of his shit. He kept saying that she wasn't going nowhere, but I guess she showed his ass," Co-Co chimed in.

"He sounded so hurt, but I understand why my sister left," Keller spoke up.

She loved Jaden like a blood brother, but she didn't blame Kia for her decision to leave him. Kia had been with Jaden for years and he had taken her through some changes during that time. It was the same thing with her relationship with Leo. She had reached her breaking point, which was why she left him and never looked back.

"Aww, he was supposed to propose to her today too," Tessa sighed, feeling genuinely hurt about what was going on.

"Girl, I forgot all about that. Bring me over there Keller. Since Jaden is depressed, I know he not gon' eat that food that Brooklyn cooked. Me and Dwight about to be eating good tonight," Co-Co said excitedly.

"Really Co-Co? Your cousin just lost his woman and you're worrying about food," Tessa said, shaking her head at him.

"I feel bad about what my poor cousin is going through, but it don't make no sense for all that good food to go to waste," Co-Co replied, like it was simple.

"You should be ashamed of yourself," Keller fussed at him.

"Should be, but I'm not," Co-Co said, poppin' his glossy lips.

"Tessa, call my man and tell him to meet us by Jaden," Keller said to her friend.

She drove towards what was now Jaden's house, to see what she could do to for her niece's father and friend.

"Girl, he's already over there. Jaden must have called him too," Tessa replied a few minutes later.

"Aww, Tigga is such a good friend," Co-Co replied. "Let me call Dwight and tell him that I'm bringing some food home."

"You are so inconsiderate Co-Co!" Keller yelled as she drove.

"Keller, bitch please. Stop acting like you're so innocent. You can lie to Jaden all you want to, but I know that Kia told you what was going on," Co-Co pointed out.

"I swear, I didn't know anything. She said that she didn't tell me because I would have told Tigga. She didn't say nothing to nobody, but I bet you that Mo knew what was up. That whole sneak move got her name written all over it," Keller replied, knowing exactly how her mother operated. Kia had definitely gone to Mo for help and that much she was sure of.

Chapter 20

"Nigga, you scary as fuck!" Leo yelled at his brother Jamal.

"You can feel how you want to feel. I'll bring you to your car and you can do whatever you want to do," Jamal said as he kept his eyes focused on the road.

Leo was still on the hunt for Tigga almost two months later. He had gone to his grandparents' house on several occasions, but he hadn't caught up to him yet. He saw Terrell's parents coming and going at various times, but he had yet to see Tigga or Tessa over there. Terrell was still adamant about not knowing where his kids were living, so Leo was ready to take it to another level. He promised Terrell that he wouldn't harm his parents, but that was a promise that Leo was not willing to keep. If putting a bullet in one of Terrell's parents would get his son to show his face, then he was willing to do that and more.

"You passed right in front of the house ole scary ass boy. I could have handled my business and been out of there in no time. The old bitch was outside working in her garden. Her back was turned, so she wouldn't have even seen me coming," Leo reasoned.

"I'm not about to help you kill no old ass lady just because her grandson got the best of you in a fight," Jamal said, making Leo even angrier than he already was.

"That nigga didn't get the best of me. His punk ass snuck me!" Leo yelled.

"From what you said, you saw the nigga coming. You just thought he was coming for Terrell, but he came for you instead. Ain't nothing sneaky about a nigga walking right up on you," Jamal said, calling him out.

"Fuck you Jamal, bruh. Just bring me to my car and I can handle this shit myself. When I finish, Terrell gon' be burying his whole family. His son played with the right nigga."

"You got issues man. Your daddy fucked you up when you lived with him," Jamal said, shaking his head.

"Nigga, don't say shit about my daddy. At least he was around. Let's talk about your crack head ass pops who stole everything that wasn't nailed down," Leo spat angrily.

"I'm not denying that, but that was all on him. Your daddy was wicked with a black heart and he raised you up to be just like him."

"You keep talking reckless and one of these bullets in this gun gon' be for your ass," Leo threatened as he lifted his shirt to reveal his weapon.

Jamal made sure to stop talking after that. Leo was crazy enough to do anything and he proved that more than once. After he beat their sister down like a dog, their mother washed her hands with him. Jamal thought that Pat was foul for turning her back on her son, but now he understood why she did it. Leo was unstable. He had no love for no one, not even himself. He did Keller wrong, now he was mad because she moved on with somebody else.

"Shit!" Jamal hissed a few minutes later, once they got onto the bridge. "Toss that gun out of the window."

"What?" Leo asked as he looked up from reading Erica's text messages.

"The police nigga. Throw that shit out of the window."

"Fuck! What's going on up here? You know I'm a wanted man."

"I don't know. Something must have happened. Hopefully, they won't worry about you since I'm the driver," Jamal responded as he watched Leo toss his gun over into the water.

"Damn man," Leo said as he nervously fidgeted in the passenger's seat.

He kept his gaze forward as his brother inched along with the traffic, until they got up to where about a dozen police cars were parked. Leo held his breath and listened as the police told his brother about a shooting that happened not too far away. Apparently, the shooter fled on foot and they were stopping everything that moved until they caught him. He felt confident about being let go when the officer handed his brother back his information. Another officer made sure that Jamal's trunk and back seat was empty, and Leo thought for sure that they were about to be let go. Regrettably, lady luck wasn't on his side that particular day. Leo wanted to jump out of the car and run when another officer requested to see his identification as well. If he didn't think he would be shot down like a dog, that's exactly what he would have done. It took the officer all of one minute to verify his info before he was walking back over and ordering Leo out of the car. Leo tuned him out as he was cuffed and read his rights. He knew the routine, so there was no need for all of the formalities. He was heated that he was headed back to that dreadful place that he never wanted to see again. But he was even more heated that his plans to deal with Tigga would have to wait for months until he reclaimed him freedom again.

***

"Yes! Shit, baby, right there," Keller moaned as she tried her best to hold on to the post of the bed. Tigga had her legs wrapped around his neck with his face and tongue buried deep inside of her hidden treasure. Keller felt like she was floating up in the clouds as he licked and sucked her dry. Her legs shook violently, but Tigga refused to let up. Keller went from screaming for him to stop, to begging him to do it again. He ignored everything that she was saying and kept going until he thought she'd had enough. Keller was so happy that he was holding her up because her legs felt like they were made of jelly when they finally hit the floor. Tigga climbed into their huge king size bed with Keller's body still wrapped snugly around his.

"Hop on top and take a ride," he instructed, once he laid flat on his back and stroked his erection slowly while looking into her eyes. She smirked at what he had just said, but she still crawled over to him and lowered herself onto his pole.

"Not too fast baby," Keller warned as Tigga thrust his body upwards to match her movements. He could be kind of rough at times, so Keller had to slow him down. She always told him that he underestimated his size, but she felt every inch of him.

"Damn girl. You putting in work, huh," Tigga hissed while smacking Keller's ass as she bounced up and down. Her long hair was wild and damp from sweat, making her look like an exotic model. Her eyes were shut tight and he was mesmerized by the cute faces that she kept making. Tigga was ready to beat it up, so he flipped her over onto her stomach and roughly entered her from behind.

"Uhh," Keller gasped when Tigga plunged into her soaking wet middle. It seemed as if she felt him in her stomach, but she loved every bit of it. She started throwing it back at him fast, until he grabbed a handful of her hair to slow down her movement.

"Stop trying to make me cum," he demanded as he smacked her ass again and watched as it jiggled.

"I thought I was supposed to make you cum." Keller smiled as she looked back at him and licked her full lips. She and Tigga stared into each other's eyes for a while, until the ringing of Keller's phone broke their eye contact.

"Who the fuck is that calling you at two in the morning?" Tigga yelled as he stopped moving and looked down at her.

"I don't know baby. Look and see," Keller replied, right as he pulled out of her and grabbed her phone from the dresser.

"I swear I love you too much to hurt you, but please don't play with me, Keller. Why is somebody calling you restricted?" he yelled while looking at the phone.

"That's probably Kia. She always calls restricted, just to make sure nobody can get her new number."

"Yeah okay," Tigga replied while looking at her sideways.

"You want me to call her back to prove it?" Keller offered.

"Nah, I believe you. Now, put that ass back in the air," Tigga said while getting behind her just like he was before.

He and Keller moaned at the same time when he reentered her. It didn't take long before they found their rhythm once again. Tigga had a handful of Keller's hair wrapped around his big hand, while he tried to break her back with his hard strokes. Keller was backing it up on him something serious, and he was ready to tap out and go to sleep. The ringing of her phone killed his vibe once again, as the restricted number flashed across her screen.

"Don't trip, it's Kia," Keller tried to convince him once again.

"Answer it," Tigga demanded while never missing a stroke.

"What? Right now?" Keller asked while looking back at him.

"Yes, right now. Unless you have something to hide," he said, giving her a look like she was lying.

Tigga had trust issues because of what Anaya did to him, but Keller was not a cheater. She tried to convince him that she was nothing like his ex, but he had to see that for himself. She had nothing to hide, so she grabbed her phone and answered, putting the call on speaker for him to hear.

"Yessss," Keller moaned into the phone, right as Tigga was hitting her spot.

"Did I wake you?" Kia asked, sniffling into the phone. Keller knew that she had probably been crying again, but that was nothing new since she had left Jaden.

"Noooo," Keller moaned once again.

"So, how was the trip? Did my baby have fun? I saw the pictures on Facebook. It looked like she had a good time. Her cake was beautiful. Where did it come from?" Kia asked, firing off a bunch of questions and statements all at once.

"Ooh shit," Keller mumbled into the pillow while Tigga hissed out something that she couldn't understand.

"Did I catch you at a bad time sis?" Kia questioned.

"YES!" Tigga and Keller both yelled out at the same time.

"Oh my God. Are y'all fucking? Bye Keller, call me later," Kia said before hanging up the phone.

"Shit, wait baby, stop moving," Tigga begged when he felt his release coming on. Keller ignored him and kept backing her ass up on him.

"Cum with me," Keller moaned, sending him all the way over the edge. A few seconds later, his seeds spilled out as he collapsed on the bed, pulling Keller down with him.

"Damn, that was good," he panted while kissing the back of Keller's neck.

"It always is," she replied while reaching for her phone.

"Damn Keller, you can at least cuddle with a nigga for a little while before you hop on the phone."

"I will baby, but I need to call my sister back first."

"Kia need to quit playing and bring her ass back home. She always calling here crying when she can just make the shit right."

"Don't talk about my sister, nigga. She just wants to know how her daughter enjoyed her birthday trip. This is the first time that she and Jaden didn't do something with Jaylynn as a family," Keller replied.

Jaylynn wanted to go somewhere for her birthday, but Jaden didn't know where to take her. When Tigga came up with the idea of Jaden and his daughter joining him and his family at his Florida rental property, he happily accepted the offer. Jaylynn was much older than Tigga's daughters, but she was happy just to have somebody to play with. She had a good time going to the waterparks and walking on the beach. She smiled the entire time they were there and that was all that mattered to Jaden. Keller found a bakery in the area and Jaden ordered her a beautiful three-tier cake. Kia took her baby girl on a spa day as her birthday treat when they came back, but it just wasn't the same as them doing something together as a family. Kia had been gone for three months now and she didn't have any plans on going back. Keller had just found out where she was living, but she would never let Jaden know. She caught Tigga trying to eavesdrop or go through her phone a few times, but she was careful to cover her tracks whenever she and Kia communicated with each other. He was trying to help Jaden out and Keller was helping her sister.

"She can have her family back if she stop being so stubborn," Tigga said, shaking Keller from her thoughts.

"I know you like Jaden and all, but you haven't been around that long to know all that my sister has been through. Jaden cheated so many times that I lost count and she always took him back. You can't pay me to believe that you've never seen him do my sister dirty since y'all have started hanging out."

When Tigga remained silent, Keller shook her head in disgust. She already knew the answer without him having to say a word. Jaden was a dog and he was getting everything that he deserved and more.

"I never walked down on the nigga fucking nobody or nothing, but that dude really loves your sister," Tigga said, coming to his boy's defense.

"But he didn't love her enough to be faithful. No matter how you put it, Jaden caused all of this. He pushed her away and now he wants to play like the victim. I won't even lie, I love his crazy ass, but I love my sister more," Keller replied honestly.

Tigga nodded his head in understanding, as Keller grabbed her phone and walked out of the room. He had to admit that she was right. As much as he liked Jaden, he was the cause of Kia leaving him. Tigga remembered Jaden's family telling him that Kia was going to get tired, but he kept brushing them off. He hated to see his boy going through it, but there was nothing that he could do. Asking Keller questions about her sister was like talking to a brick wall. Even playing detective when she wasn't around didn't help. She erased anything from her phone that had to do with Kia, so that was a dead end. Jaden was so stressed out that his weight was dropping like crazy. The only thing that seemed to make him happy was the time that he spent with his daughter. Other than that, he stayed inside all day if he wasn't at the shop. He tried asking Jaylynn about where Kia lived, but she only told him that it was far. She couldn't explain it, so he gave up on asking her.

"Okay, I'm done," Keller said when she came back into the room a few minutes later. Tigga smiled as he pulled the covers back for her to get into the bed. He pulled her body close to his as they laid there in complete silence, both lost in their own thoughts. That was, until he tapped her leg to signal that he was ready for round two.

Chapter 21

Anaya sat on the bench at the playground with her girls and wiped a few stray tears as they fell from her eyes. She scrolled through the pictures on Tessa's Facebook page and got sick to her stomach. She couldn't believe that Tigga had Keller and whoever those other people were with him at his vacation property in Florida. She only felt sicker when her daughters informed her that they went there for Keller's niece's birthday. That explained the other little girl that was in just about every picture that was posted. Tigga must have really be feeling Keller to be doing something so extravagant for one of her family members. He barely even knew any of Anaya's family and he seemed determined to keep it that way. She felt stupid for thinking that having Tigga's kids would be enough to keep them together. So many times he'd offer to pay for her to go back to school, but she always declined. He even offered to give her a job at his construction site, but Anaya wasn't interested in working. She got comfortable with him always taking care of her, but she regretted that and so much more.

"Are we going by our daddy today?" Tia asked as she ran up and scared her mother half to death. Anaya hurriedly hid the bottle of Hennessey that she'd been sipping on back inside of her hobo bag.

"No, this is my weekend to keep y'all," Anaya slightly slurred.

She was never much of a drinker, but she'd been so stressed out lately and she needed to numb the pain. Not only was Tigga and Keller's relationship weighing heavily on her mind, but she hated the apartments that she was now living in. They weren't bad at all, but it was much smaller than she would have liked for it to be. She loved the place that she and Tigga had before because she had lot of extra storage and closet space. She felt like the new placed was too crammed and she hated it. Not to mention how trifling Rich was. She had never lived with him before, but he was a complete slob. He left clothes and dishes all around the house, and she felt like she had four kids instead of three. Tigga was a neat freak, so that was so new to her. Rich still hadn't had any luck finding a job and he barely contributed to the bills. Anaya was over it and it was only a matter of time before he would be getting his walking papers.

"Aww man, I wanted Keller to make us some ice cream sundaes," Tia said right before she ran off to join her sisters on the swings.

"Fuck Keller," Anaya mumbled as she pulled out her bottle and took another swig. She hated when her kids mentioned Keller, but they seemed to love the little slut just as much as their father did. Anaya should have been happy that her kids liked their father's girlfriend, but she hated Keller too much to care. Many times, she wanted to show up at their house and beat her ass for the stunt that she and Tessa pulled, but she didn't want to have to deal with Tigga. He didn't think that Anaya knew where they lived, but the courts had his address printed on just about every page of her child support documents. Anaya passed around there a few times, but the armed man standing guard at the front gate was the only reason that she never attempted entry.

"Mama, it's boring. Can we go to the zoo or something?" Tia asked as she and her sisters ran back over to her.

"We don't have any money for the zoo. Your daddy didn't give me any," Anaya said as she drank an ice cold bottle of water that she had pulled from her bag in an attempt to sober up. It helped her out a lot, but her depression was still at an all-time high.

"Call him, he'll give us some money!" Tia yelled excitedly.

Anaya wanted to yell at them to leave her alone, but it wasn't her kids' fault that she had fucked up her life. It really wasn't Tigga's fault either, but she still blamed him for leaving her. The fact that he moved on and was happy with another woman was tearing her up inside. She remembered happier times when he would give her a stack of money and tell her to go enjoy her day, while he stayed home with the kids. When they moved into their first house together, he let her pick out all of the furniture and decorate any way that she wanted to. She was genuinely happy with him until Rich came back into the picture. She took Tigga for granted, thinking that he would always be there because of the kids. Now she was stuck in a relationship with the bum ass nigga that she cheated on him with.

"Mama!" Tia yelled to get Anaya's attention.

"What girl?" Anaya asked as she looked over at her kids.

"Are you gonna call our daddy for some money?" her daughter questioned.

Feeling a little liquid courage from the Hennessey had Anaya ready to take it a step further. "I'm not calling him. I'm going over there," Anaya said as she stood up and sluggishly walked over to her car.

She knew that she shouldn't have been driving, especially with her kids in the car, but her common sense was long gone once she started drinking. The excited cheers from her girls further proved to her that she was doing the right thing. She slowly drove away from the park and towards where Tigga and Keller's house was located. Against her better judgement, Anaya still sipped from her bottle, not caring that her children were watching. She felt her car swerve every now and then, but she managed to make it to Tigga's house in one piece. She hid her bottle of alcohol and frowned when she saw the security guard standing at his post when she turned in, but her girls seemed to be happy about it.

"Hey Mr. Henry!" Tia rolled down the window and yelled.

"We're going to see our daddy!" Talia yelled just as loud.

"Hey pretty girls," the security guard said, smiling at them. He always saw the girls coming in and out with their father and they made it their business to speak to him every time they came through. To Anaya's surprise, the man went into his little booth and opened the gate up for them to enter. He even waved them through with a smile as they passed him by.

"Dumb ass," Anaya mumbled as she pulled out her bottle and chugged it until it was all gone. The bottle wasn't huge, but it was enough to give her double vision when she finished it. She was tipsy as hell and right on the verge of being completely wasted.

"That's the wrong way. My daddy goes the other way to get to his house!" Tia yelled, once they were inside of the gated community.

"Okay, wait a second," Anaya slurred. She pressed on her brakes hard and slowly turned her truck around to go in the opposite direction.

"Ooh mama, you made that mirror come off of that car," Tia yelled as Anaya knocked the side mirror off of a white Charger that was parked on the street.

"So," Anaya snickered as she went the way that her girls told her to go. Although she had Tigga's physical address, she didn't know which one of the properties he lived in. Anaya was driving on lawns and everything else, trying to get to her destination. Her girls were holding hands, scared to death that they were going to crash.

"Right there!" Tia yelled when they got to the townhouse that belonged to her father. Anaya jumped the curb and pressed on her brakes hard, making the girls almost fly into the front seat. Amari and Talia were crying, but Tia jumped out of the truck as soon as it came to a complete stop. She was young, but she knew that something wasn't right with her mother. She told her sisters to follow her as they ran up to Tigga's porch and rang the doorbell.

"What the fuck," Tigga mumbled to himself when he looked out of the window and saw his kids standing there. The tear stains on Amari and Talia's faces had his heart beating faster than he needed it to. When his eyes landed on Anaya's truck that had jumped the curb, he instantly knew that something was wrong.

"Mama knocked somebody's mirror off of their car. She was driving on the grass and everything. I think something is wrong with her," Tia said as soon as Tigga opened the door.

"Stop crying and come inside. Y'all go to your room while I see about your mama," Tigga instructed.

"Don't leave her out there, daddy. She gon' die," Tia begged.

"You gon' bring her inside daddy?" Talia said while wiping tears from her eyes.

"Yeah, just go upstairs to your room and wait for me," Tigga replied.

He was happy as hell that Keller was out spending the day with Tessa and Kia. She would be acting a fool about Anaya showing up to their house if she was home. He didn't even know that Anaya knew where he lived, but that was beside the point. Tigga walked up to the truck and immediately got pissed off when he looked inside. Anaya was clearly drunk and the empty bottle of Hennessey sitting in the passenger's seat was proof of that. She was a stupid bitch to be drinking and driving with her kids in the car with her. He was happy that they were safe, but he was still upset that it happened. Tigga was tempted to leave her ass sitting right out there, but he couldn't do that to his kids. They were still peeping out of the window, trying to make sure that their mother was okay.

"You got your bitch living nice in a gated community," Anaya slurred when Tigga opened the door to help her out of the truck. She was mumbling all kinds of foolishness about him and Keller, as he held her up and walked her into the house.

"She's alright, y'all take Amari upstairs and watch tv," Tigga said to his daughters, who were standing there watching Anaya laugh and act a fool. He waited until they walked up the stairs and closed the door before he dropped Anaya right on the tiled floor.

"Ow!" Anaya yelled as she hit the floor hard.

"Stay your drunk ass right there on the floor too," Tigga said as he walked into the kitchen.

He had just purchased Keller a turquoise and chocolate brown leather sofa set and he refused to let any part of Anaya's body touch it. It was bad enough that she was in his house at all. Although Keller had planned to be gone all day, Anaya still needed to be on her way out. Tigga grabbed a bottle of water and watched Anaya drink it all the way down. Having had a few hangovers before himself, Tigga knew that something hot would probably help too. Keller had some kind of fancy coffee machine that he couldn't work, so he decided to make some hot tea instead.

"Where are my kids?" Anaya asked a few minutes later, as she held her head with both of her hands to control the throbbing pain. The room felt like it was spinning around her and vomit was threatening to come up from her belly.

"The fuck you worried about them for now? You didn't think about them when you were driving drunk!" Tigga yelled.

"Stop talking so loud," Anaya said while closing her eyes.

"This is my fucking house. Matter of fact, you need to call you a cab or a ride so you can get going. I don't need my girl coming home to see this shit," he replied as he gestured towards her sitting on the floor.

"My mama is out of town and I don't have money for a cab. Just give me a minute and we'll be out of here."

"Who is we? I hope you don't think your drunk ass is taking my kids nowhere. You can kill yourself, but they won't be with you."

"I have to take Amari home with me," Anaya mumbled.

"You think I give a fuck about how your other baby daddy feels? Where was that nigga at when you were driving around sipping from a bottle of Hennessey with your kids in the car?" Tigga snapped, making tears fall from Anaya's eyes.

He was right and she felt like a damn fool for even being there. Reminiscing about the past, coupled with drinking, really had her in her feelings. She would have never showed up to his house if she were in her right mind.

"I'm so sorry for coming here Tigga. I don't know what's wrong with me," Anaya said as she held her head in her hands and cried.

"I don't know what's wrong with you either, but you better get it together. I don't want to have to take my kids from you, but I will. This drinking and driving shit is unacceptable. You could have killed yourself and them too," Tigga said while handing her an ice cold towel and a cup of tea. Anaya felt a little better, but she still didn't feel comfortable enough to drive.

"I know Tigga. I swear that this will never happen again. I've just been going through it lately and I fucked up," Anaya replied through the pain in her head.

"Yeah, well you can sit there and get yourself together for a few minutes, but you have to go soon. I'll bring them to you later when you sober up," Tigga said, right before he walked away to go check on the kids.

Anaya looked around his house and admired the furniture and decorations that accompanied them. The color scheme in the living room was beautiful and she knew, without a doubt, that Keller was the one who put it together. Tigga was content with a bed and a tv, so he really didn't care about stuff like that. Anaya was green with envy as she looked at all of the pictures of Tigga and Keller that lined the walls. They seemed so happy with each other and that's what she hated the most. She knew, without a doubt, that Tigga gave her the world because he'd done the same for her when they were together.

"You should feel good enough to be on your way now," Tigga said when he walked back into the room with another ice cold bottle of water that he handed to her. Anaya was about to tell him that she did, but the jealous side of her wanted Keller to come home and find her there. She wished she was there when she first showed up because she would have loved to see her face.

"Uh yeah, but can I use your bathroom right quick? I feel sick," Anaya said, trying to play on Tigga's sympathies. He looked skeptical about granting her request, but he gave in eventually.

"Make that shit quick Anaya," Tigga said as she stood up and slowly walked to the door that he pointed to. Anaya closed and locked the door behind her and smiled to herself. She wasn't in a hurry to leave, so she pulled the lid down on the toilet and took a seat.

"Shit," Tigga sighed as he grabbed his phone to call Keller. He needed to make sure that she wasn't on her way home because there was no way that he could explain Anaya being there. The more he thought about it, he decided not to call Keller at all. He decided to call Tessa instead because she was the only one who could help him out.

Chapter 22

"Man, I hate to see y'all go. When are y'all coming back?" Kia asked as she walked Keller and Tessa outside to the car.

"Bitch, you live too damn far. What the hell made you move all the way to Luling?" Tessa argued.

Kia was renting a nice three-bedroom house in a gated subdivision in Luling, Louisiana. She and Jaylynn had their own rooms and she used the third room for her office space, since she now worked from home. She had the place decorated beautifully and she was proud of what she had accomplished on her own. She had left Jaden's debit card back at the old house, so she did everything with the money from her own savings. He couldn't take credit for anything because she made it all happen without him.

"Girl, Mo found this place for me, but I love it. The rent is cheaper here then it was at my old apartment. When I buy a house, I want to get one right out here," Kia replied.

The night that she called Mo crying over Jaden, her mother jumped right into action. She asked Kia if she was really ready to leave and she promised her that she was. That was all that Mo needed to hear before she started house hunting on Kia's behalf. She loved Jaden, but she loved her daughter more. If he wasn't doing right by Kia, then he needed to keep it moving.

"Now I see why Jaylynn never told her daddy where you live. Poor baby probably can't even explain it. This is over thirty minutes away from where y'all used to live," Keller said.

"She told me that he asked her a few times, but she be lost her damn self. She said that it's too confusing getting back here. You know it looks like a maze," Kia said laughing.

"She's so happy that she got her an iPhone now honey. She be calling and texting me all day." Keller smiled.

"You know I be calling her from a restricted number too. His ass is always grabbing the phone, trying to talk to me. It's sad that my baby can't even have my new number because of him, but that's his own fault." Kia frowned.

"He be coming to work looking so pitiful. It's not even fun no more, since him and Co-Co don't be going at it all the time. It's like he don't really talk to nobody that much no more," Keller added.

"That's all on him. He should be wilding out since I'm not there to hold him back. I'm doing me and Jaden is nowhere on my mind," Kia replied.

"Bitch, stop acting like you don't be calling, crying me a river all the time," Keller said, calling her out.

"Don't do me that Keller. Jaden is all that I've ever known since I was a teenager. Of course I get in my feelings every now and then, but that doesn't mean that I want his ass back. I just get a little depressed sometimes when I think about it," Kia replied.

"So, when am I gonna meet your new boyfriend?" Keller asked her sister.

"He is not my boyfriend. We've only been on three dates. He doesn't even know where I live. We always meet up at the post office where he works," Kia replied.

Kia had a post office box for her mail and she had trouble opening it one day. The manager, a cutie named Darius, assisted her and they ended up talking for hours after that. He was easy to talk to and they exchanged numbers before she left. He had been begging Kia for a date before she finally agreed to go. It had been so long since Kia had to do the dating thing. All of that felt new to her and she was nervous as hell. Thankfully, Darius understood her position and made her feel very comfortable with him. They went to dinner and a movie on their first date and she really enjoyed herself. So much so that she agreed to do it twice more after that.

"Well, I still wanna meet him," Keller requested.

"And guess who called me?" Kia smirked.

"Who?" Keller asked.

"Andre. You remember the one who Jaden beat up that time?"

"Yeah, but how did he get your number?" Keller inquired.

"He called me on my work cellphone. He said that he heard that Jaden and I weren't together anymore and he wanted to take me out. Probably one of my so called friends at the hospital told him all of my business," Kia frowned.

"What did you tell him?" Keller asked.

"That nigga got a golden tongue, so I told him that I'll think about it." Kia laughed.

"I hope you don't tell Jaylynn about him or your post office man. Jaden is gon' be on his Rambo shit if you do." Tessa laughed.

"It's not even that deep for my baby to meet or even know about them. I have to be damn near walking down the aisle before I introduce Jaylynn to anybody. You can't trust some of these men these days," Kia reasoned.

"And you're right sis," Keller noted.

"You all in my mix, but what's up with you and Ryan?" Kia asked Tessa.

"Not a damn thing. I just took his ass off the block list yesterday. He's on some let's start over shit, but I'm not about playing no games," Tessa replied.

"Starting over is a good thing. That means that he doesn't want to lose you," Kia said.

"Maybe so, but it ain't nothing for me to cut a nigga off. I've been celibate for three years now. I'll be damned if I break my celibacy to fuck a nigga while his mama is in the bed holding his hand," Tessa said, making the sisters laugh.

"And on that note, I'm gonna let y'all go," Kia said as she held her stomach from laughing so hard. Tessa didn't give a damn what she said or when she said it.

"Yeah, we need to get going. I need some gas to make it back home from way out here in this country," Tessa joked.

"By y'all, love you, sis!" Kia yelled.

"Love you too!" Keller yelled out of the window as they pulled away from the house.

Although she missed seeing her sister several times a week like she normally did, Keller was so proud of her. Making a move from Jaden wasn't easy, but Kia did what she had to do. It had been a few months since she left and she seemed genuinely happy. She was starting to date again and she needed that in order to move forward.

"You want something out of here?" Tessa asked Keller when she pulled up to the gas station.

"Anything chocolate. It must be getting close to my time of the month," Keller replied.

"Me too girl. That's all I've been wanting," Tessa said when she got out and walked towards the entrance. She hadn't even gotten through the door good before her phone started ringing, displaying her brother's number and picture. Keller smiled as she picked up the phone, preparing to mess with him.

"Uh-huh," Keller mumbled with a smile covering her face. That smile immediately faded when Tigga started to talk.

"Aye, I need you to make sure that Keller don't come home right now. I know y'all are around each other, so don't say it's me. Don't even ask no questions; I'll explain it to you later," Tigga rambled before he disconnected the call.

Keller's heart sunk as she tried to fight the tears that were threatening to fall. She didn't know what was going on, but it had to be something that he didn't want her to find out about. She felt stupid for putting Tigga on a pedestal when, in reality, he turned out to be just like every other nigga who did wrong. She really wanted to believe that he was different, but her gut was telling her that he was a dog just like the rest of them. Keller sat there in a daze, as Tessa threw a bag of chocolate candy in the car and pumped the gas that she had just paid for. Tessa didn't even pay attention to Keller's distant behavior as she drove to her house where Keller's car was parked.

"Let me know when you make it home boo," Tessa said when Keller got out of her car.

"Okay, I will," Keller promised as she got into her car and sped all the way home. She wasn't sure what she was going to walk in on, but the suspense was killing her more than anything. Her heart was fluttering in her chest to the point of almost having an anxiety attack. Keller had never experienced that feeling before, not even when she was with Leo. When she pulled up to the gate, Mr. Henry smiled and opened it up for her to drive through. Keller drove in the direction of their townhouse, holding her breath the entire time.

"That dirty muthafucker!" she hissed angrily when she pulled up and saw Anaya's truck parked in front of their door. It was more like it was jumped up on the curb, but it was there nonetheless. Tigga had given Keller her gun back and she was tempted to pull it out of her glove box and walk in the house shooting. She promised herself that she would use the weapon responsibly, and Tigga nor Anaya were even worth a bullet. She just had to see what was going on for herself before she overreacted or assumed. She got out of her car and looked inside of Anaya's vehicle, just to make sure she wasn't in there. Once she saw that the car was empty, she already knew what was up. Keller's hand shook nervously as she inserted her key into the door and pushed it open. She heard the kids laughing upstairs, but somebody was also moving around in the kitchen. She braced herself for what she was about to walk in on, but she visibly relaxed when she saw Tigga standing over the sink washing dishes. That nigga had ordered pizza, wings, and everything else to entertain a bitch that he swore he couldn't stand anymore. When he looked up and saw Keller standing there with her arms folded across her chest, he already knew he was in some deep shit.

"You care to explain to me what your baby mama's truck is doing outside," Keller said with an angry stare.

"Baby, I swear it's not even what you think. She drove over here drunk with my kids in the car-" Tigga started explaining until Keller cut him off.

"How does she even know where the hell we live?" Keller yelled angrily.

"I don't know. She just showed up drunk with the kids in the car," Tigga answered honestly.

"Well, I hope she parked her car and took a cab home," Keller said while staring at him. She knew that it was wishful thinking, but she just didn't want to believe that he was dumb enough to let a bitch who hated her step foot inside of her comfort zone. Tigga looked like he was at a loss for words, but Keller had was just getting started.

"Please tell me that bitch is not still here Tigga," Keller said as she closed her eyes to calm herself down.

"Baby-" Tigga said before she cut him off again.

"Tyler I swear, if I go upstairs and your baby mama is in one of those bedrooms, I'm fucking you up, no questions asked," Keller fumed as she walked away from him.

"Just listen to me Keller. She's not upstairs. She's in the bathroom. I've been telling her that she had to leave for over an hour, but she claimed that she's too sick to drive. I even offered to pay for her a cab. I promise, it's nothing like you think it is," Tigga tried to explain.

"You sound stupid as fuck! Nigga, I was the one who answered Tessa's phone when you called and begged her not to let me come home right now. All that because you're trying to creep with your baby mama. You should have just stayed with the gutter bitch when you had her," Keller fumed.

"I don't fucking want her!" Tigga yelled back, right as Anaya walked out of the bathroom. His mouth hit the floor when he saw how she looked. Her hair was all over her head and she was holding the jeans that she once had on in her hands, leaving her wearing nothing but a shirt and underwear.

"Maybe she didn't get that memo. I'll have my uncles here tomorrow to get my shit. I'm done," Keller said as she turned around and bumped into Anaya on her way out the door.

"What the fuck?" Tigga yelled angrily as he chased after Keller. "Baby, wait!"

"If you come anywhere near me, I'm pulling out my gun and shooting your dog ass," Keller threatened as she hopped in her truck with him still running behind her. She almost ran over his foot when she wildly backed out of the driveway and sped off into the street. Tigga was heated, as he ran back up to his house and straight into Anaya's trifling ass.

"I need something to throw on. I threw up all over my pants," Anaya mumbled while looking down at the floor.

"Bitch, I wish you would have choked on it and died with your no good ass. Get the fuck up out of my house. This is what a nigga gets for having a heart and trying to be nice to your rat ass!" he yelled as he grabbed her arm and forcefully pulled her out of the front door.

"Tigga, wait! I don't have any pants on!" Anaya yelled as she tried to hold on to the front door to keep from being thrown out of it.

"I don't give a fuck. It don't look like shit is wrong with the ones in your hands," he replied while tossing her onto the concrete.

"Ahh!" Anaya yelled in pain as she scraped her legs and arms on the ground. She jumped up like it was nothing and ran up on him again. "Give me my kids or I'm calling the police."

"Call them and make sure you tell them how you drove them over here drunk out of your mind," Tigga noted.

"Don't get mad with me because that hoe broke up with you. It ain't my fault that she's insecure," Anaya taunted as she put on her jeans that were clean and free of vomit. Her mission had been accomplished and she didn't care if Tigga never spoke to her again. He and Keller were no more and that was her goal from the start.

"You went through all of that and for what? I don't give a fuck if me and Keller never get back together; I don't want your nasty ass no more. You and your other baby daddy are made for each other. A hood rat and a broke lame. Nigga can't even afford to keep a few dollars in your pocket to catch a cab. Stupid ass bitch probably using your kids' child support checks just to keep a roof over your head. Get your basic ass from around here before I call my girl back over here to shoot you for real," Tigga spat as he wiped the smirk right off of her face.

He slammed the door in her face and left her standing there looking stupid. Anaya felt lower than she'd ever felt before, mainly because Tigga was right. She was using the child support that he gave her to take care of her kids, herself, and Rich. Hearing him actually say it out loud only made the situation seem worse. After walking to her car and getting inside, Anaya broke down crying at what had become of her life. No doubt she was the reason for the way that it turned out, but that still didn't make her feel any better. Anaya wiped her eyes and started up her truck, preparing to go home. She looked up just in time to see Tigga rushing out of the house with her girls, probably going to chase after Keller. Once he had them all strapped in, he turned and made eye contact with Anaya. When he mouthed the words "get the fuck on bitch" to her, she put her car in drive and left him in her rearview. Tigga had called Christy and asked her to keep the kids while he tried to go talk to Keller. He couldn't let the night end with her still being upset with him. She was talking about moving out, but there was no way that he could let her do that either, especially since he didn't do anything wrong.

Chapter 23

"I can't believe this shit man. Two whole weeks and she still not trying to come back to a nigga," Tigga said as he smoked and talked on the phone with Jaden.

Keller was stubborn as hell and she didn't want to hear nothing that Tigga had to say. She was done playing the fool for any man and that included him. She sent Mo and her uncles to get her belongings from Tigga's house and she had been living with her mother ever since then. Tigga even tried talking to her at the shop, but he was just like a stone wall to her; something that she saw, but paid no attention to. He tried to play on her sympathy by telling her that the girls wanted to see her, but that didn't even work. Keller got Tessa to get them from his house and she took them somewhere on her own. Tigga now knew exactly how Jaden felt because he was sick without Keller.

"Shit, nigga, I believe it. You see how long Kia ass been gone, huh? Got me feeling like a love sick bitch out here," Jaden replied.

"But I didn't even do shit. I'm being punished for nothing. I should have at least got some head or something since I'm already being accused of cheating," Tigga fumed.

"You my boy and I love you like a brother, but you know what your problem is bruh?" Jaden asked him.

"What's that?" Tigga inquired.

"Your ass is too damn nice. It's like you're a thug with a heart and that shit just don't mix," Jaden replied.

"So, my girl packed up her shit and left me because I'm too nice," Tigga repeated sarcastically.

"You playing, but that's exactly why she left you. I can

understand you being worried about your kids and all, but your baby mama would have been on her own. Once you got your girls inside safely, you should have let that bitch drive off and commit suicide. Fuck you care about her for anyway, after what she did to you?" Jaden asked angrily.

"It wasn't about me caring about her. Man, my kids were crying, begging me to bring her inside. They knew that something was wrong and they stood there and watched me the entire time. That shit messed with me to see them looking like that."

"Man, I wish I could help you, but I'm fucked up myself. Mo raised some stubborn ass daughters," Jaden replied.

"Mo be on that shit right along with them. She came through my house like she pay bills up in that bitch when it was time to get Keller's stuff." Tigga laughed.

"Mo is as gangsta as they come. She'll do anything for her daughters, no doubt about that. I know that she was the one who helped Kia move out on me. That's how she operates. She do shit when you least expect it. She be nice and silent with it."

"I went to her house to talk to Keller and she wouldn't even let me in. She pretend like she like a nigga, but she left my ass standing right there on the porch."

"That don't mean she don't like you. If Keller told her not to let you in, then she wasn't letting you in. She's down for her daughters. Simple as that," Jaden told him.

He knew Mo well enough to know how she maneuvered. There were plenty of times where he was left standing on the porch, so he knew just how Tigga felt. Once he and Kia made up, she was back to same old Mo that he knew and loved. It was always personal with her when it came to her daughters and she let everybody know it.

"What you getting into tonight?" Tigga asked Jaden after a long pause.

"Not a damn thing. I'm just pulling up to my mama's house. Mo came picked up Jaylynn to bring her by Kia, so I'm on my own. I swear, I hate when my baby don't be at home."

"I feel you, bruh. I don't have my kids either. I'm going chill with my grandpa for a while. I hate being at home by myself now, so I might crash on their sofa. Hit me up tomorrow so we can go have some drinks and finish crying," Tigga suggested.

"Bet." Jaden laughed, right before hanging up the phone.

It was a little after nine that night, but Jaden knew that his parents were still up. They usually didn't go to bed until after midnight, even though they both had to be to work at seven every morning. After opening the front door, Jaden disarmed the alarm system and made his way upstairs to his parents' bedroom. They heard him come in, so none of them were alarmed when he appeared in the doorway. Pam was propped up in her bed on some pillows reading a book on her iPad, while Bryce Sr. laid next to her reading the newspaper. Jaden kicked off his shoes at the front door and walked over to them. Bryce Sr.

already knew the routine. Jaden came over to their house every time Jaylynn went to spend time with Kia. He pulled the covers back and got out of the bed, preparing to go relax downstairs in his favorite recliner. Pam put her iPad down and patted the spot in the bed that her husband had just vacated. Jaden was hard in the streets, but he was still her baby. Brooklyn was the youngest of them all, but Jaden was Pam's baby boy. He would never let anyone see the side of him that he so willingly showed to her. He had no guard to keep up with her and he didn't even try. There was just something about his mother's love that he just could not do without. Jaden climbed into bed with his mother and welcomed the warmth of her wrapping him up in her embrace. He felt like a vulnerable little boy and Pam always knew just how to comfort him.

"It'll get better baby," Pam said as she rocked Jaden in her arms and let him cry into her chest.

"This shit feels like it's getting worse. I don't think she's ever coming back," Jaden sobbed shamelessly.

"You have to give her time Jaden. I know without a doubt that Kia loves you, but she was tired. I can't tell you what it'll take to get her back, but you need to be patient. Maybe being alone for a while is what you need. Get yourself together before you rush her to come back," Pam suggested.

"I'm already together. She's been gone for months and I ain't even looked at another bit... woman," Jaden said, correcting himself before she did. Pam always fussed at him for calling women bitches, especially since he had a daughter and other women in his life that he loved.

"You should have been doing that while y'all were still together. I keep telling you that whatever is meant to be will be. A few months won't take away the years of hurt and pain that you put her through."

"You still on my team though, right? It sounds like you're switching sides on me," Jaden said while looking up in his mother's eyes.

"It's not about sides or teams, Jaden. You're my son, but I'm also a woman and I have to keep it real with you. You're a man whore and that's why Kia left you. I pray for y'all every night, but God does everything in his own time. You can't rush that," Pam replied, making him nod his head in understanding.

"I'm just scared that she gon' move on and be with somebody else. I can't take that ma. You already know how I am when it comes to Kia. Even Jaylynn seems to be adjusting to these new living arrangements."

"What's meant to be will be Jaden. Stop stressing over something that you can't change or control. And Jaylynn is a child. She's happy just to spend time with both of her parents. To be honest, my grandbaby needed a break from all that drama between you and Kia."

"I guess," Jaden sighed in defeat.

"Have you been eating Jaden? You look like you're wasting away. You have to take better care of yourself baby. I cooked some cabbage and baked chicken. Come on downstairs so I can fix you a plate," Pam suggested as she gently tapped his arm for him to get up.

Jaden got up and followed his mother downstairs, bypassing his father who was sitting in the front room.

"What's up?" Jaden said while taking a seat on the sofa that faced his father's recliner.

"I can tell you what ain't up and that's your overgrown ass sleeping in the bed with me and my wife," Bryce Sr. snapped.

"Man, it ain't like nothing is going on with y'all," Jaden said, waving him off.

"I guess not if your cry baby ass always coming over here getting in the bed with us. They got all these extra rooms in here, so you better pick one to sleep in. Fuck with me and I'll have your mama in the room screaming right next to your ass," Bryce warned.

"Aww man, come on. Don't nobody wanna hear about you and mama having sex," Jaden said as he jumped up and walked away to answer his ringing phone.

"Nigga, how you think you got here," his father said before he walked out of the room.

"What's up Pluck?" Jaden asked.

"I'm on that bitch bruh!" Pluck yelled as soon as Jaden answered the phone.

"You on who?" Jaden quizzed.

"That bitch Tori. Me and my sisters were on Claiborne at the Wingstop and I saw her," Pluck replied.

"Damn bruh, did she see you?" Jaden asked. "She gon' know what's up if she did."

"Nah, I never got out of the car. I'm following her ass right now. I got three of my sisters with me so this is the perfect time."

"Damn right it is. Tell them I got some extra cash for whoever get the most licks in."

"Bet, I'll get at you as soon as everything is handled," Pluck said right before hanging up.

***

"Ugh! I can't wait to get back on my feet. I need my own damn house," Tori vented to no one in particular.

She was on her way back to her Aunt Donna's house with Anna and her broke ass man. She had to pay him gas money, just to bring her to get something to eat because Donna rarely had food in the house. Her aunt worked a lot or visited her man in Mississippi whenever she had the time. She always made sure that she had food when her grandkids came over, but that wasn't very often. Tori hated that she was back in the trailer park, but she didn't have anywhere else to go. She stayed with one of her friends off and on, but that got old fast. Anna lived in the trailer park too, but she lived on the other side. Her side of the park wasn't as nice as the one that her mother lived on, but she kept a clean house. The rent was dirt cheap, which was why she moved from her mother's trailer to one of her own.

"You need to rent you a lil one-bedroom trailer for a little while. You keep saying that you don't wanna live in the trailer park, but you really don't have a choice. What's the difference between you living with my mama or having your own?" Anna questioned.

"I don't wanna be back here at all. I'm not knocking y'all or nothing, but trailer park living just ain't for me," Tori spat right as they pulled up to the front entrance of the park. Anna's man must have been in his feelings because he didn't even drop Tori off in front of the door where he picked her up from.

"I'll talk to you later miss high and mighty," Anna said sarcastically, right before they pulled off and left Tori standing there.

"Miserable bitch," Tori mumbled as she walked the short distance to her aunt's trailer. She was almost to the front door when she heard what sounded like glass and leaves crunching under someone's feet. No one really hung out in the trailer park too late, so Tori was curious to see who was walking around so late at night. She made the mistake of turning around and was met with a brass knuckled fist to her face as soon as she did. The leaves and grass crackling on the ground was nothing compared to hearing the bones in her nose crack from the blow.

"Oww!" Tori screamed out in pain as she dropped her food to the ground and grabbed her burning and bloody nose. She instantly went down to the ground, when three chicks that she'd never seen before started hitting her in every visible part of her body. She didn't know what was worse. The pain in her nose or the shooting pain that her body felt after every strike.

"Oh God, please," Tori cried and begged for mercy from the most high. She needed help and no one else was able to do it, but Him.

"Don't beg now bitch. Did Kia beg when y'all jumped her?" one of the women asked, even though she had never met Kia a day in her life.

Tori really got scared when she mentioned Kia's name. She knew, without a doubt, that Jaden would be gunning for her, but she wondered how he had found out where she was. Aside from her sister, Toni, he didn't know anything about anybody else in her family. Now, she was questioning if her sister had given up some info that she never should have mentioned. Toni was scared to death after they kicked her door in, so maybe she did run her mouth about some of Tori's possible whereabouts.

"Are we supposed to kill the bitch or just beat her ass?" one of the women asked, making Tori beg and plead for her life. Her eyes were almost swollen shut and she was barely moving, but that didn't stop them from their brutal attack. She wondered who the women were that Jaden had obviously paid a lot of money to do the deed. They were definitely earning however much it was that they were being paid and more. Her fight with Kia wasn't even that serious for him to go to such lengths.

"That's enough, the bitch ain't even moving no more. We keep this up and she will die," another angel said. Tori didn't even know who she was, but she had to be an angel to come to her rescue and stop them from committing murder.

"She's fucked all the way up." One of them laughed as they ran away just as fast as they had come.

"Mmm," Tori moaned in agony as tears spilled from her badly beaten, swollen eyes. There was no way that she could move to get help, so she prayed that somebody found her and got her some help soon. Sadly, she knew that it probably wouldn't be until morning.

Chapter 24

"Fuck my life!" Keller sniffled as she sat on the bathroom floor at Kia's house and cried.

"Oh my God! I'm so excited. I'm gonna be an auntie," Kia yelled excitedly.

"What the hell are you so happy for? This is not the right time for me to be having a damn baby?" Keller snapped.

"You should have thought about that shit before you started having unprotected sex. And whatever happened to you taking the birth control shots?" Kia questioned.

"I missed one," Keller mumbled. "Maybe two."

"Well, you can wipe those crocodile tears boo. You weren't handling your business, so welcome to motherhood," Kia replied.

"That bitch at the clinic told me that the medicine stays in your system for a while even if you miss a shot."

"None of that matters Keller. You're pregnant, so that was obviously not true. You need to make you an appointment to see how far along you are. When was your last cycle?" Kia asked.

"I don't know; I have to check my calendar."

"You don't know!" Kia shouted. "Was it that long ago?"

"No, maybe a month or two, but that's not unusual with the shot. Ugh! I'm just not ready for this," Keller whined.

"You think I was ready to become a mother while I was still in high school? Things don't happen when we want them to Keller. I didn't protect myself and Jaylynn was the result of that. She was a blessing and I don't regret one thing about having her though."

"Yeah, but at least you and Jaden were still together. Me and

Tigga broke up and I haven't talked to him in over two weeks," Keller replied.

"And what does that have to do with the life that's growing inside of you? The only reason that you and Tigga aren't speaking is because of you. I watched you ignore at least ten calls from him since yesterday. Why is that when you said you know that he was being truthful?"

Keller still hadn't talked to Tigga, but he ran the entire story of what happened down to Tessa. Even his kids told their auntie what happened and their story was almost identical to the one that Tigga had given. Christy was pissed about Anaya drinking and driving with the kids in the car, so she called to confront her. When Tessa told Keller how Anaya cried and apologized for what she did, she felt stupid for not believing her man. She was too stubborn to tell him that, so she kept up the mad act longer than she intended to. Not only that, but Keller was starting to have doubts about a lot of things.

"I don't know Kia. I'm starting to wonder if me and Tigga moved too fast. I love him, but I don't wanna keep getting hurt. I look at what I went through with Leo and what you went through with Jaden, and I don't want to be that girl," Keller said after a long pause.

"Don't do that Keller. Don't compare Tigga to Jaden or Leo. He's never cheated or put his hands on you, so that makes him different from both of them. Stop being so scared and stubborn. You really need to talk to him now more than ever," Kia advised.

"Why can't I just be happy? Even Tessa and Ryan are doing better and trying to make something happen between them," Keller revealed.

"Everybody wants to be happy sis. It just doesn't happen like that all the time. It's unrealistic to think that you'll never have problems in a relationship. You just have to know how to deal with it," Kia replied.

"How? By running away from it like you did?" Keller asked.

"I didn't run, I left. You and I both know that I would have given in to Jaden had I stayed or let him know where I was. He was my weakness, so leaving was best for me. Don't get me wrong, I'm still in love with him; I just can't be with him. I was losing me in the process of loving him."

"I understand what you're saying Kia, but I don't know why I always get these no good ass men in my life. I do my part in the relationship, but I always get fucked over," Keller noted.

"Tigga didn't fuck over you, but I understand why you were pissed. The fact that his baby mama was in your house at all is enough to make you go off. Then, the bitch took her pants off to make you think that it was more than it really was. He should have been smarter about how he handled it, but I don't see him as a cheater. You really need to have a serious talk with him."

"I'll answer for him the next time he calls. I guess I need to get this conversation over with anyway. But don't you tell anybody until I'm ready Kia. Promise me," Keller said, looking over at her sister.

"Okay, I promise. Now, let's go feed my niece or nephew before you go back home. Mo is gonna be so excited to get her another grandbaby." Kia smiled.

"I know she is. Now, I know why I've been craving chocolate like crazy. I thought it was because my cycle was about to come on."

"Girl, just wait. Those cravings are gonna drive you crazy, especially if you can't get your hands on what you want," Kia warned.

"I wonder if Rachel will make me some brownies with chocolate frosting. Ooh, maybe she'll make me a chocolate cheesecake," Keller said as she pulled out her phone to call her cousin. Rachel was a Pinterest queen and she mastered every recipe that she came across. She could cook and bake anything, just by looking at the ingredients.

"Poor Tigga. He gon' have to buy you a chocolate fountain or something." Kia laughed while grabbing her purse to leave.

Keller hadn't even left yet and Kia was missing her sister already. Keller spent the weekend with her, but she had to get back to work the following day. Kia was praying that things between Tigga and Keller worked out because she knew how her sister felt about him. He was good for Keller and even Mo had to admit that. They had never seen her so happy or smile so much.

"I wonder why I don't feel sick or nothing like that," Keller wondered.

"Don't question it, just be thankful. Jaylynn had me throwing up water and all when I was pregnant with her," Kia said as she locked up her house and walked to the car. She and Keller were taking separate cars, so that Keller could go home afterwards.

***

"Hello," Tigga said in shock as he looked at the phone. He couldn't believe that Keller had finally answered for him after weeks of being ignored.

"Yeah," Keller said, sounding like she was sleeping.

"Did I wake you?" Tigga asked, happy as hell that she answered.

"No, I was just laying here," she replied.

"I'm surprised that you even answered, but I'm happy that you did. We really need to talk Keller. I don't want you to think that I'm out here doing you dirty. That shit ain't even me," Tigga swore.

"Okay," Keller agreed.

"Okay what?" Tigga questioned.

"I'll come over there after work tomorrow so we can talk," she promised.

"Cool, what time?" he asked.

"Um, I don't know. I'll call you when I get off from work. We shouldn't be that busy."

"Are you coming back home to stay?"

"I don't know Tyler. We'll talk about it when I see you tomorrow."

"Man, I hope you do. I miss the fuck out of you," Tigga admitted.

"I miss you too," Keller said honestly.

"Do you still love me?" he asked her.

"Of course I still love you, Tigga. Feelings don't just go away when a person is upset. That's unrealistic," Keller replied.

"I love you too, baby." Tigga smiled for the first time in a while.

Chapter 95

"Thank you so much Rachel. I can't wait to dig into my sweets," Keller said to her cousin over the phone.

"You're welcome cousin, and congrats on the pregnancy," Rachel replied.

"Thanks Rachel, but please don't tell anybody. I haven't even gone to my fist doctor's appointment yet."

"I only told Gary, but you know he won't say anything," Rachel said, referring to her boyfriend who Keller was also cool with.

"That's fine, but don't tell anybody else," Keller begged.

"Okay, I won't," Rachel promised. "But I gotta go cuz. My break is over. Gary should be there any minute with your stuff."

"Okay boo, call me later," Keller said before they disconnected the call.

It was crazy how Mo had lots of brothers and sisters who had kids, but she and Kia weren't really close with any of them. They saw each other at family functions and it was always a good time, but they never really stayed in touch. Most of them lived in New Orleans, so there was really no reason why. Mo was tight with her brothers, so she saw her nieces and nephews quite often. There was never any bad blood with the cousins and they were always genuinely happy to see each other. Keller was happy that she and Rachel were spending more time together and she wished that she could do the same with her other cousins.

"What you in here doing?" Mo asked when she and Robert walked into the house and found Keller lying on the sofa.

"Nothing, I'm waiting for Gary to bring me something that

Rachel made for me. Hey Mr. Rob," Keller said, speaking to the older man who was with her mother.

"Hey my baby," Robert said, walking over to hug her.

Robert had been Mo's on and off boyfriend for years since Kia and Keller were teenagers. It was rumored that he was ruthless in the streets and the drug game some years ago, but he was a changed man. He now owned just about every house on the block that Mo lived on, including the one that she was in. That was before he signed the five bedroom, three bath home over to the younger woman who had long ago stolen his heart. Mo didn't want for anything and he made sure of that. He was ten years older than her at fifty-six years old, but he didn't look a day over forty. Kia and Keller loved to see him get dressed up because he did it so well. He'd been damn near begging Mo to walk down the aisle with him, but she wasn't really feeling the idea. When their father, her first love, died years ago, Mo had given up on the possibility of happy endings. Fairytales were only for storybooks, as far as she was concerned. She wanted that for her daughters, but she had given up on love for herself. Mo's heart had turned cold to relationships and marriage, but Robert had her second guessing that at times. It was easier for her to break up with him and be with other people than it was for her to face her reality. She was in love with him and it scared her to death. He was always so good to her and her girls, and she couldn't have asked for a better man. Rob was the one who put both of her girls through college and she would be forever grateful to him for that.

"I might be sleeping out tonight," Keller informed her mother.

"Sleeping out where?" Mo asked with raised brows.

"I'm going talk to Tigga later and I might stay there until tomorrow," Keller replied.

"It's about damn time. I'm so sick of hearing you play that depressing ass music all day." Mo laughed right before she and Robert walked away.

Keller laughed too because she was sick when she and Tigga had broken up. She listened to every break up song imaginable, from K. Michelle to Fantasia and lots of others. Mo fussed at her just about every day because she was sick of hearing it. Hopefully, things would work out between her and Tigga because she was sick of playing them.

"Coming!" Keller yelled when somebody rang the doorbell. She got excited because she knew that it was Gary with her sweets.

"Hey mommy to be." Gary smiled when she opened the door to let him in.

"Boy hush," Keller said, looking behind her to make sure that the coast was clear. "You know you can't be saying that out loud. Come on and bring my stuff in the kitchen."

"Sorry cuz," Gary said as he walked in and followed her to the kitchen.

Keller didn't waste any time before she grabbed a fork and dug right into her chocolate cheesecake. Gary laughed when she closed her eyes and savored the flavor of the sweet treat.

"Damn, I love my cousin," Keller said as she bit into the chocolate frosted brownie next.

"Girl, you gon' have the shits all night after eating all that chocolate," Gary joked.

"It'll be so worth it too," Keller replied.

"It's always nice to see you cuz, but I gotta go. I just wanted to drop that off to you, but I'm still on the clock," Gary said as he walked to the door.

Keller followed him out and down the steps to his awaiting cab. She laughed to herself when she thought back to their first interaction. Gary was the driver of the cab that she called to pick her up one night when she and Leo had gotten into a fight. She was so terrified of cabs that she took a picture of his plates and sent it to Kia. Keller remembered grilling him like she was a detective, as he drove her to her sister's house. It was really funny when she found out that he was her cousin's boyfriend. She and Gary had been cool ever since and he was actually a nice person. He and Rachel had been dating for two years and they made a cute couple.

"Tell Rachel that I said thanks. She'll be hearing from me for something else soon, but I'm sure she knows that," Keller said as she stood outside and talked to Gary.

"She'll be hearing from you for the next couple of months. Do you know how far along you are?" Gary asked.

"No, I haven't gone to see a doctor yet. I'm sure that I'm no more than a month or two though," Keller replied.

"What about the baby's daddy? Does he know?"

"Not yet, but I'm meeting up with him tonight to tell him."

"I hope it's not the crazy one with the hand problem," Gary said, referring to Leo.

He and his girlfriend had to pick Keller up from a gas station once because she ran out of the house after Leo beat her.

"Hell no! I haven't been with him in about a year or so," Keller replied with a frown.

She was so happy that she hadn't heard from Leo in a while. Maybe he was served with the eighteen month long restraining order and decided to stay his distance. Maybe, he had found himself another woman to abuse like he had done to her for so many years. Whatever the reason was, Keller was just happy that he was out of her life.

"That's good, but we'll catch up later. Let us know when you see the doctor or if you need anything," Gary said as he and Keller hugged.

"Okay Gary, thanks." Keller smiled as she watched him get into his taxi and pull away. She went back into the house to feed her face some more, before heading over to Tigga's house. She packed a bag, just in case things between them went well and he wanted her to stay.

Chapter 26

"These hoes just can't be trusted," Tigga mumbled to himself as she started up his grandmother's car and sped away from Mo's house.

He was so happy that he and Keller were on the right track to getting back together. He took the day off from work and decided to wash clothes and give the house a good cleaning. He had his grandmother to cook a pot roast with potatoes and vegetables for them to eat when she came over. While the meal was being prepared, Tigga decided to take his grandmother's car to get washed. He thought about Keller the entire time that he was at the detail shop and he couldn't wait any longer to see her. They had talked on the phone for a while earlier, but that wasn't good enough. Deciding to pop up at Mo's house to surprise her, he got a surprise of his own when he turned the corner. Keller was leaned up against a cab, smiling in some nigga's face like it was cool. Tigga parked right at the corner that he'd just turned and watched them talk for a while. His heart dropped to his stomach when he watched the woman that he was in love with hug another man right before his very eyes. Mad was an underrated emotion compared to how Tigga was feeling. He sped to his grandmother's house and parked her car in her driveway. Tigga wanted to drop her keys on the table and leave, but she had his food packed up and ready for him to take.

"You're just in time baby. You and Keller can keep these containers. I got enough of them already," Mary said, handing Tigga some bags with the containers in them.

"Alright grandma, thanks," Tigga said as he took the bags and prepared to leave.

"What's wrong baby?" Mary asked while stopping him from walking away. "You didn't even give me a kiss."

"My bad," Tigga said as he kissed her cheek and left her standing in the kitchen.

After throwing the bags in his truck, Tigga sped all the way home, lost in his own thoughts. He was happy as hell that he had something to drink and smoke inside because he needed them both. He didn't want to believe that Keller was doing him dirty, but he had to admit that the scene that he'd just witnessed didn't look good. Maybe that was why she wasn't in a hurry for them to get back together. That also explained why she offered to come to him, instead of asking him to come to Mo's house. Maybe she didn't want her side nigga to pop up and see that Tigga was there. All kinds of thoughts were running through his head and none of them were good. Keller being intimate with another man damn near turned his stomach inside out. As good as the food in the bags smelled, Tigga didn't have an appetite. He hopped out of his truck and threw the bags of food in the trash before letting himself inside. He hated that his grandmother wasted her time cooking, but it was going to go to waste anyway.

"Yeah," Tigga said as he answered his phone for Tessa. He was pouring himself a drink and getting ready to light up right when she called.

"Save me some of that food that grandma cooked for you and Keller," Tessa begged.

"I don't have no more," Tigga replied honestly.

"Stop lying Tigga. Grandma told me that you just left right before I got here. She just cooked it for you, so I know it's not gone that fast."

"The food is gone Tessa. Fuck I gotta lie to you for," Tigga snapped in anger.

"Don't get crazy with me. If you don't want me to have none, just say no," Tessa argued.

"If you want it, come dig in the muthafuckin trash can and get it!" Tigga roared before hanging the phone up in his sister's face.

Thanks to Keller, he was in a bad ass mood and it probably wouldn't get better any time soon. He was tempted to call and tell her not to come, but he needed her to know that he saw what she was up to not too long ago. There was no way that he was about to let her think that she got away with doing him wrong. She made his life a living hell for weeks when she thought that he was still fucking Anaya, but she was out there doing some foul shit herself. Tigga felt bad for snapping on his sister, but he wasn't in the mood to apologize just yet. He needed to handle the situation with Keller before he did anything else. He wouldn't be able to eat or sleep until he did.

***

Keller was a nervous wreck as she pulled up to Tigga's house. She was happy that they were finally going to talk and put their problems behind them, but she also wondered how he was going to take the news of her pregnancy. He already had kids and they had never discussed if he wanted more or not. She knew, without a doubt, that Tigga would be a great father because he already was. He admitted to some mistakes that he'd made in the past being a first time father, but he was great with his kids now.

"Yes Kia." Keller smiled when she answered the phone for her sister.

"Did you tell him yet?" she yelled excitedly.

"No girl. I just got here a minute ago. I didn't even get out of the car yet," Keller replied.

"Why? Are you nervous?" Kia asked.

"Yeah, a little," Keller answered honestly.

"I don't know why. He's gonna be so happy. Maybe you'll give him his first son."

"I hope not. I want a girl."

"You don't need no girl sis. You can't comb hair for shit," Kia joked.

"Shut up Kia. You learned how to do it and so will I." Keller laughed.

"I guess, but I gotta go get ready for my date. Sneak off and call me and let me know what he says," Kia ordered.

"Okay, I will. Have fun," Keller said before hanging up the phone and getting out of her car.

She left her overnight bag in the car, since she didn't want to seem too eager. If he wanted her to stay, then she would send him back out to get it. Keller tried to shake her nervousness as she opened the door and let herself inside of the house. She didn't know why she kept her key after she moved out, but giving it back just made her decision to leave seem so permanent. The potent smell of weed accompanied by a thick cloud of smoke greeted her as soon as she walked in. That struck her as odd because Tigga usually smoked on his patio and away from her and his girls. He also didn't want the weed smell to linger in his house, especially because his daughters were always over there. Keller ventured deeper into the house and found Tigga in his den, posted up on his black leather sofa. He had a half empty bottle of Cîroc in his hand, while a few empty beer bottles littered his feet. The room was dark, but the light from the tv was enough for her to see everything.

"Hey," Keller spoke when she walked into the room and took a seat in the recliner that sat next to the sofa. Tigga looked over at her and turned the bottle up to his mouth without bothering to speak back. He was so happy earlier when they spoke, but now it seemed like she wasn't even welcomed there.

"Is everything okay? What's up with all the drinking?" Keller asked him.

"Ain't shit up with it. I'm grown," Tigga snapped with a scowl.

"I know you're grown Tigga. I just asked a simple question."

"And I gave you a simple answer," he flippantly replied.

"Okay, I don't know what the problem is, but it's obvious that something is wrong. You asked me to come over here and talk, but I guess it'll have to wait," Keller said as she stood to her feet, preparing to leave. She was happy that she didn't bring her overnight back in with her. There was no way in hell that she was spending the night with him and that nasty ass attitude.

"I didn't ask you to come over here, you offered. We ain't got shit to talk about anyway. I'm good on you and this relationship," Tigga replied.

"You're good on me?" Keller repeated as she pointed to herself in shock.

This couldn't possibly be the same nigga who had been blowing up her phone for weeks begging for another chance. Not the same Tigga who showed up to her job and her mama's house damn near every day almost, crying for her to talk to him.

"That's what I said," he stated with a disgusted look on his face.

Keller didn't know what was wrong and she really didn't care. She wasn't in the business of begging a man to be with her. She couldn't lie though; her feelings were hurt by how he was talking to her. Tigga was never ugly with her, but obviously things had changed. Keller was questioning if she should tell him about the pregnancy or not, but she decided that she didn't want to wait. Maybe hearing about the pregnancy would soften his heart and make him feel better about whatever was bothering him.

"That's cool Tyler, but I have to talk to you about something. I'm not saying this for us to get back together or nothing, but I feel like you should know. I took a pregnancy test yesterday and it came back positive. I haven't seen a doctor yet, so I'm not sure how far along I am," Keller said while looking over at him.

She expected him to at least smile or say something when she delivered the news, but he sat there and kept his focus on the movie that he was watching. He didn't even turn his head to face her or acknowledge her presence. Keller spoke loud enough for him to hear her, but she decided to repeat herself just to be sure.

"Did you hear what I said Tigga? I'm pregnant," Keller repeated.

"Fuck you telling me for? Go tell your baby daddy," Tigga spat angrily, making her sick to her stomach.

"What?" Keller whispered in shock.

"You heard me. Go tell that bum ass nigga whose face you was smiling in and hugging on earlier!" he yelled.

"What nigga? What are you talking about?" Keller asked in confusion.

"So, you gon' stand here and play crazy Keller?" Tigga asked as he jumped up and towered over her.

"I ain't playing shit. I'm trying to see what the hell you're talking about!" she yelled.

"So, you wasn't in front of Mo's house with some nigga who drives a cab. Smiling in his face and hugging him and shit. But I couldn't even get you to answer the fucking phone for me."

"Gary? Are you seriously standing here accusing me of fucking my cousin's boyfriend?" Keller yelled.

"Oh, so that's your story?" Tigga asked as he laughed sarcastically.

"What fucking story? That's the truth," Keller swore with tears in her eyes.

Now, she knew what the problem was. Tigga must have been at Mo's house when Gary was there. All he had to do was walk over to them and he would have had his answers right then and there. Instead, he chose to play little boy ass games and assume shit instead.

"I'm not trying to hear that shit man. Go tell that nigga that you're pregnant. I'll be damned if I let another bitch put a baby on me that ain't mine," Tigga said, ripping her heart from her chest. There were no words in the English language that could describe how Keller was feeling at the moment. She was done and there was no doubt in her mind about that.

"Fuck you!" Keller managed to say through her tears. She pulled his key from her ring and tossed it at his feet as she rushed off towards the front door. Regret engulfed Tigga as soon as she left, but his pride refused to let him run after her. He wanted to be happy about her being pregnant, but thoughts of how he had been played by Anaya wouldn't let him. Once he heard Keller's tires screeching off, Tigga flopped back on the sofa and continued to smoke.

***

"Fuck him!" Kia fumed as she hugged her sister while she cried.

When Keller called and told her what happened, she immediately cancelled her date and waited for her to come over. She couldn't believe how Tigga had played her sister and she was pissed.

"That bitch ass nigga had the nerve to say go tell my baby daddy that I'm pregnant. Like I wasn't fucking his ass every day for almost a year. Fuck him. I don't him or his baby. I'm making an appointment bright and early in the morning," Keller swore.

"Now you're going too far. I'll get a bigger house so we can all live together, but you're not getting no damn abortion."

"That's not for you to decide Kia. This is my body. I don't want no parts of Tigga and that includes his baby. I'm not Anaya. I'm not having a nigga's baby just to keep him around. I'll bounce back from this shit just like I do with everything else."

"Please don't get an abortion Keller. I'll take the baby and raise it myself if you can't do it. I'll do whatever I have to do. Just please don't take things that far," Kia begged.

"I need to get some rest for work in the morning. I'm sorry that you had to cancel your date," Keller said, changing the subject.

"Girl please," Kia said, waving her off. "If he don't understand that my family comes first, then fuck him too."

"Was he mad that you cancelled?"

"I don't know and I don't care. I sent that nigga a text message." Kia laughed.

"Damn." Keller laughed with her.

"But, anyway, we need to make you an appointment with Dr. Mullins. You know Mo will want you to see the same doctor who delivered us and Jaylynn," Kia pointed out.

"I'll pass." Keller frowned. "Dr. Mullins is like two hundred years old."

"Stop over-exaggerating. He's a good doctor and that's all that matters," Kia said.

Keller only nodded her head, but she wasn't trying to see any doctor unless he specialized in abortions. She didn't feel like going back and forth with Kia, but her mind was already made up. She didn't want anything to do with Tigga and she meant that. Keller loved Tessa like a sister, so she prayed that her decisions didn't put a strain on their friendship. She knew that things would be a little awkward for her, but she would just have to adjust. After all, it was her brother's fault how everything went down anyway.

Chapter 27

Tori had just gone to bed a little over three hours ago and she was up already. Rich and Anaya had been up early arguing, once again, and she was sick of hearing it. Since she didn't have anywhere else to go, she really didn't have a say in the matter. It had been a little over a month since she was beaten within an inch of her life. Tori had suffered a broken nose and a long list of other injuries. Thankfully, someone coming home from work a few minutes later discovered her and called an ambulance. She thought that she was going to be in the driveway all night, but she was rescued from her agony. She stayed in the hospital for over a week before she was able to go home. Her sister, Toni, had poisoned her Aunt Donna's mind and she was too scared to let Tori come back to live with her. Anaya had just started a new job at the airport, so she offered Tori a place to stay in exchange for watching her kids. Tori had the same deal with her sister Toni, so she jumped at the change. Besides, Anaya's apartment complex was ten steps above living in the trailer park. The area was nice and she felt comfortable being there. The only problem was the constant bickering that went on between her and Rich. Anaya was pissed that she was the only one working and paying bills, while Rich barely contributed.

"Hello," Tori said as she groggily answered the phone for Serena. They had been in contact a lot lately and she was helping Tori keep some cash in her pockets.

"Can you make a few runs for me today? If you can find a ride, you can make three hundred dollars real quick," Serena offered.

"That nigga still ain't find nobody to help you out?" Tori

asked, referring to Jaden. Serena didn't know the situation about Tori fighting Kia and Jaden having her jumped in return. She still thought that Jaden didn't fuck with Tori because she had caught feelings for him and Tori didn't tell her any differently.

"Girl, no, and it don't look like he wants to. Don't get me wrong; the money is lovely, but I got kids to spend time with. I can't be doing this shit twenty-four seven. I be in the room bagging this shit up and have to lock my kids out," Serena complained.

"You doing the shit at your house now?" Tori asked in shock. Usually, Jaden would rent a room for them to handle stuff like that. He must have really trusted Serena to let her bring his product to her house.

"I don't have a choice. I would be spending too much time away from home if I didn't. My baby just got over the flu. I wasn't leaving him with nobody while he was sick. I haven't even been bringing Jaden his money. He must not want it because he never came to get it either," Serena said, talking all over herself.

She had the wheels in Tori's head turning like crazy. Jaden would die if he knew that Serena still had Tori handling his business, but she needed the help. After what he had done to Tori, she had something in store for his ass and it wasn't gonna be pretty.

"What time you want me to come through?" Tori asked her.

"It'll be a little later. I'm waiting for my mama to come get my kids, so I can really put in some work. I'll call you as soon as I'm ready. You gon' have a ride?" Serena asked.

"Yeah, I will," Tori promised her.

"Okay, I'll call you later when I'm ready," Serena said before they disconnected.

Tori hung up the phone with a huge smile plastered on her face. Serena was the dumbest bitch that she had ever met. She had unknowingly helped Tori cook up a plan to get Jaden back in more ways than one. She may have thought that Tori was coming to get a few bags of pills to distribute, but Tori wanted it all, including the money. She wanted Jaden's life taken away from him too, but hitting his pockets would have to do for now. Having him killed and taking his money was even better, but she had to have somebody crazy enough to do it. She knew for a fact that if Jaden didn't die, there would be hell to pay. Tori only had a few hours to come up with a master plan, but that wasn't hard for her to do. She knew more about Jaden than he thought and she was gonna use that to her advantage.

When Tori heard the front door slam, she knew that her cousin had left for work. She was happy because she was tired of hearing Anaya and Rich scream back and forth at each other. She was also happy because she didn't have to babysit. It was Tigga's time with the kids, so Tori was free to do whatever.

"I'm so sick of this shit," Rich fussed when he walked pass the room that Tori slept in. The door was slightly opened, probably by one of Anaya's kids before they left. All of the girls slept in one room, but they had toys all throughout the house, including the room that she slept in. Tori threw the covers back from her body and got out of the bed. She slipped her feet into her slippers and made her way into the kitchen where Rich was seated.

"Good Morning," Tori greeted when she walked in and opened the refrigerator.

"Hey," Rich grumbled in anger.

"Damn. Who pissed in your cereal?" Tori chuckled.

"Man, I'm really getting sick of your fucking cousin. She act like a nigga ain't out here busting my ass every day looking for a job. She so used to what that other nigga did for her and she's expecting me to do the same shit. My money ain't long like his, so she can get that shit out of her head," Rich fussed.

"Don't even try to compete with Tigga. That nigga got money that he'll probably die before he spend and he's making more every day," Tori replied honestly.

"Fuck that dude. I'm not trying to compete with him and nobody else. I'm just trying to find a way to help her pay some of these bills and keep her off of my ass," Rich replied.

"I can probably help you out with that if you're down," Tori offered.

"How can you help me with anything when you're basically in the same boat as me? We both live here and can't afford to contribute shit," Rich chuckled.

"Nah nigga, speak for yourself. I pay my way by babysitting, but if my cousin needs my help financially, I got her," Tori replied.

"Where do you get money from? You barely leave the house," Rich observed.

"That's what I'm trying to explain to you. The chick that I used to hustle with be needing my help from time to time. She wants me to fall through later tonight to pick up some pills."

"And how do I fit into the equation?" Rich inquired.

"You can come with me and do your thing," Tori replied.

"You mean rob her?" he asked, just to be clear. He was ready for whatever, but he needed to make sure that they were on the same page.

"Exactly. She just told me that the dude that she hustle for hasn't picked up his money in a while. She got dope and money, and she'll be home by herself," Tori informed him.

"But she know you though, right? She might tell dude your name and shit," Rich said, trying to make sure he wasn't getting in over his head.

"Let me worry about all that. Are you in or out?" Tori asked.

"How much money are you talking about?" he questioned.

"I don't know, but it's usually a couple of thousand. It's enough to get my cousin off of your ass for a while. But I'll do you one even better." Tori smiled.

"What's up?" Rich asked attentively.

"I know where the dude live at who she hustle for. He got even more money than that at his house," Tori lied. She knew that Jaden never kept anything at home around Jaylynn and Kia. She just needed Rich to go with her while she put a bullet in his head.

"So, you wanna get at him instead of her?" Rich asked.

"We can do both. She's an easy target, but we might have to catch him slipping," Tori reasoned.

"Man, I don't know about that. I feel like I'm going into this blind. I don't know shit about these people and how they operate."

"I know everything that we need to know. You want Anaya off of your ass or not? I'm trying to give you a chance to walk away with a nice bit of money. You can help out for a few months with that. Plus, you can have some pills to sell if you want to," Tori noted, trying to sweeten the deal even more. Rich rubbed his goatee as he thought about everything that Tori was saying. He had to admit that the offer sounded too good to pass up. Anaya had been on him a lot lately and he knew that the money would be a big help to her with the bills

"I'm in," Rich said, making Tori smile from ear to ear.

Chapter 28

Serena flopped down on her bed, exhausted from the events of the day. After her mother picked her kids up, she finished doing what she had to do before cleaning her house from top to bottom. After making a few drop offs, she grabbed something to eat and went home to wait for Jaden. She had over twelve thousand dollars hiding in her closet for him and she was happy that he had finally come to pick it up. She hated holding on to his money for too long because she didn't want to be held responsible if anything happened to it. Now, she was waiting for Tori to pick up the last few bags of pills that she had left and drop them off to the awaiting customers. She was too tired to do anything else but take a shower and go to bed.

"Coming!" Serena yelled to who she knew was Tori ringing her doorbell. She was tempted to meet her at the door with the pills because she really didn't want to be bothered. Tori asked too many damn questions and she really wasn't in the mood to deal with her.

"What's up?" Tori asked as she stepped inside of Serena's house and looked around suspiciously.

"Not a damn thing. I'm tired as hell," Serena replied, not paying attention to Tori's unusual behavior.

"You having company or something? You got it clean as hell up in here," Tori wondered.

"Bitch, my house is always clean. Let me go get this shit for you," Serena said as she left and walked to the back of the house.

That was perfect timing for Tori. She used that opportunity to unlock the front door and send Rich a text message. She wanted him to make sure the coast was clear and run up in there as soon as it was.

When Serena walked back into the living room with the bag, Tori frowned at the amount of pills that she was holding.

"Girl, I know this ain't the lil bit of pills that you need me to drop off. You could have done that shit yourself," Tori complained.

"I dropped off most of them earlier, but I'm tired as hell now. And stop complaining, it ain't like you doing the shit for free," Serena said as she handed her three crisp hundred dollar bills. Tori was about to reply when the front door burst open and Rich came running inside. Serena looked like she was about to run, until a gun pointed in her face halted her movements.

"Bitch, don't even think about it!" Rich yelled at her. "Where the money and the dope at?"

"I don't have no money or no dope," Serena said as warm tears cascaded down her cheeks. Nothing like that had ever happened to her before and she was scared to death.

"Don't make me pull this fucking trigger and blow your brains out. Where's the money?" Rich yelled again.

"My purse is in my bedroom. You can have it," Serena cried.

"That's really how you wanna play it Serena?" Tori asked as she pulled out a gun of her own and pointed it at her. "You know damn well we ain't looking for no purse. Where's the money and the rest of the pills?"

"I don't have anything else. Jaden picked his money up and we sold all the pills and weed. The only money I have is in my purse. I can't believe that you're doing this to me Tori. All I ever did was try to help you," Serena sniffled. She knew that something was up. She specifically remembered locking the door once she let Tori in. She must have unlocked it for her accomplice when Serena went to her bedroom to get the pills.

"Shut up talking to me and bring me to your bedroom," Tori said as she pressed the gun to her side. Serena slowly walked them to her bedroom and pointed to her purse. Rich immediately snatched it up and started rummaging through it. When he saw a knot with a few big faces sprinkled in it, he smiled, but Tori was heated.

"Fourteen hundred dollars fam," Rich said as he raised it up like that was a lot of money.

"That's it?" Tori yelled angrily.

"I swear to you that I don't have anything else," Serena promised.

"Watch her while I look around," Tori said to Rich, right after he stuffed the money in his pockets.

He pointed the gun right at Serena's head while Tori ransacked her apartment. She went through closets, drawers and flipped mattresses, but she still came up empty. Tori couldn't believe that she had done all of that scheming for fourteen hundred dollars and a few bags of pills. Jaden would pick the day that she planned to rob him to pick up his money from Serena. Knowing him, the money was probably already half spent on Kia or deposited into one of his many bank accounts.

"Fuck!" Tori shouted as she walked back into the room and paced the carpeted floors.

"I told you that I didn't have anything," Serena sneered. Her fear had been replaced by anger at how Tori had just tried to rob her. She really liked Tori at one time, but Jaden was right. That bitch was certifiable. She looked like a lunatic, pacing back and forth mumbling all kinds of crazy shit under her breath.

"Now what?" Rich asked impatiently. They had already spent too much time in Serena's apartment and he was ready to go. Obviously, the money that Tori was looking for wasn't there, but at least they had something. Fourteen hundred dollars was better than nothing at all in his eyes. They would still be walking away with seven hundred dollars each.

"I don't know. Just let me think," Tori said as she continued to pace.

"Just let it go Tori. Jaden is already gonna be gunning for your ass when he finds out what happened tonight," Serena spoke up.

"How is he gonna find out?" Tori asked as she turned to face her.

"How do you think he's gonna find out? I'm telling him!" Serena yelled.

"I doubt it," Tori replied as she raised her gun and fired a shot into the center of Serena's forehead.

"Oh shit!" Rich exclaimed as he watched Serena's lifeless body fall to the floor and stain her carpet with her still warm blood. "What the fuck Tori!"

"I told you to let me worry about her. You didn't honestly think that I would let that bitch live did you? That would have been like committing suicide if I did."

"Man, let's get the fuck up out of here," Rich said as he ran back towards the front of the house to the front door with Tori following close behind him. They looked out of the front door and around the complex, before they jogged to the beat up car that Rich was driving and got in.

"We got one more stop to make," Tori announced as they drove off and away from the scene of the crime.

"You must be out of your fucking mind. I'm bringing my black ass right home and pray that the police don't come looking for me!" Rich yelled back.

"Did you not just hear what Serena said?" Tori questioned.

"When? Before you put a bullet in her forehead?" he shot back angrily.

"Listen, the dude Jaden is the other hit that I was telling you about. Didn't you just hear her say that he picked up all the money? That nigga got the money that we were looking for. I'm telling you, Rich; five minutes is all we need to be straight for a while."

"You said that shit about the first house that we went to and your crazy ass ended up killing somebody," Rich argued.

"You know what? Fuck it! I'll do the shit on my own and keep all the money. Don't try to come crying to me when Anaya put your broke ass out of her house. How long do you think she's gonna be happy with seven hundred dollars? Tigga used to spend more than that on her shoes," Tori said, knowing just the right buttons to press.

Rich talked a lot of shit, but he was intimidated by Tigga. He always said that Anaya compared him to her children's father, but it was actually Rich who did all the comparing.

"Man Tori, we gotta be in and out. No more of that trigger happy shit that you just pulled with ole girl. And this time, we're wearing a mask. I was dumb as fuck for not wearing one the first time," Rich argued.

"Cool, we can wear a mask," Tori said with a smirk.

Rich didn't know it, but he was going on yet another bogus mission. Aside from pocket money, Jaden didn't keep a lot of cash on him. Tori really didn't want his money. The shit with him was personal. Mask or not, he would be able to spot her from a mile away. She hoped like hell that his daughter wasn't there, but she would never hurt her if she was. As for Kia, she planned to leave her in the puddle of blood right next to her man.

***

"Daddy, are you gonna go on a date?" Jaylynn asked Jaden as they drove home from Brooklyn's house. Usually, she cried to stay there, but she wanted to spend time with her father.

"I went on a date tonight," Jaden replied with a smile.

"You did? With who?" she asked him.

"I went on a date with you. I took you shopping, to a movie, and out to eat. I even let you come with me to my family's house. That's a date girl," Jaden joked.

"No daddy, I mean a real date like mama be going on," Jaylynn said, almost making him lose control of his car.

"Who did your mama go on a date with Jaylynn?" Jaden questioned.

"I don't know, but my Tee Keller asked her how was her date and she said she had fun," Jaylynn said, repeating the conversation that she overheard her mother having with her auntie.

"And what else?" Jaden quizzed.

"Nothing, but she said that she was going on some more dates." Jaylynn shrugged innocently.

"Not if I kill the nigga first," Jaden mumbled.

"What did you said daddy?" Jaylynn asked.

"Nothing, I didn't say nothing baby. Are you sleepy?" Jaden asked her.

"No, can we watch some movies and eat ice cream?" she questioned.

"Anything you want baby." Jaden smiled right as he pulled up to their house. He popped his trunk and got Jaylynn's shopping bags out to bring inside.

"I can't wait to show mama my new stuff." Jaylynn smiled as she used Jaden's keys to open the door, since his hands were full. Jaden smiled back at her as they made their way inside. He dropped her bags to the floor as he turned on the front room lights. As soon as Jaden turned to close the door, two masked figures ran inside with guns pointing at his head.

"What the fuck?" Jaden questioned as they barged inside and slammed the door shut.

"Give it up nigga!" a man yelled while pointing a gun in his face. Jaden wanted to laugh because the nigga looked nervous as hell, even with the mask pulled down over his face.

"Daddy!" Jaylynn yelled as she ran to his side.

"It's alright baby. Don't be scared," he said, even though he knew his baby was scared to death. He tried his hardest to keep Jaylynn away from stuff like that, but they came to their house with the bullshit.

"Where the dope and money at nigga?" Rich yelled as he looked around the nicely decorated house.

"Dude, you must be an amateur. I know damn well you couldn't have been watching this house. If you were, you would know that no dope or money come through this bitch, ever," Jaden replied calmly.

"Nigga, you must think this is a game!" Rich yelled again. Jaden ignored his scary ass and focused on the other person that he was with. That time, he couldn't hold in his laughter even if he wanted to.

"Tori, you stupid as fuck. How you try to rob a nigga and got a charm bracelet with your name dangling from your arm?" Jaden laughed.

"Fuck you!" Tori spat as she removed the mask from her face.

Rich wasn't taking his mask off. Whoever the dude was that they were robbing seemed official. The nigga wasn't even scared when they ran up in his house and that said a lot.

"My dude, I hate to inform you, but this bitch got you on a straight up dummy mission. She mad because I stopped fucking her and had some chicks beat her ass for coming at my girl wrong. Take her love sick ass up out of here. Maybe then, I might forget that y'all came to my house and scared my baby half to death," Jaden ordered calmly.

"I'm not going nowhere. And if you don't want your daughter to see you get killed, you better send her to her room," Tori said with a crazy look in her eyes. Jaden wasn't scared of anything, including death, but he didn't want his daughter to witness whatever was about to happen to him.

"Baby, go to your room and wait for me to come get you," Jaden ordered Jaylynn, who was clinging to his legs.

"Daddy, no. I don't wanna leave you. I don't want you to die," Jaylynn cried as she held him tighter. It broke Jaden's heart to see the look of fear in her eyes, but he was at a disadvantage. He had several guns around the house, but none that he could put his hands right on.

"Do what your daddy said and go to your room," Tori told Jaylynn, who looked at her like she was crazy.

"No!" Jaylynn shouted back. "Don't tell me what to do!"

"I said bring your spoiled ass to your room," Tori gritted as she pulled Jaylynn by her shirt.

"Bitch, you ain't that damn crazy!" Jaden yelled as he slapped her hard across her face, making the gun drop from her hand. He grabbed Tori by her neck, lifting her off of her feet. He was heated as he tried to choke some sense in to her crazy, deranged ass. "You better not ever put your hands on my fucking daughter."

"Rich," Tori choked out as she reached out for him to help her.

"Nigga, let her go before I shoot you!" Rich yelled as he cocked the gun back.

"Shoot him," Tori pleaded as she clawed at Jaden's hands.

"I said let her go!" Rich yelled once again. Tori couldn't believe that he was standing there continuously making idle threats, while he had a damn gun in his hands.

"I. Can't. Breathe," Tori strained to say. "Rich, shoot him."

Thankfully, he finally listened and send a bullet rippling through Jaden's shoulder.

"Ah fuck!" Jaden yelled as he dropped Tori to the floor and held his burning shoulder.

"Daddy!" Jaylynn cried as she dropped down to the floor with him and laid her head on his chest.

"Baby, go to your room and call your uncle Bryce," Jaden whispered to her. Jaylynn nodded her head as she ran to her bedroom and locked the door behind her. As soon as Tori sucked a little air into her lungs, she grabbed her gun from the floor and aimed it at Jaden once again.

"Let's go Tori! Fuck the money!" Rich yelled nervously. He was dumb as hell if he still thought it was about money, but Tori let him have that. She was ready to go too because she was sure that somebody had called the police. There was no way in hell that she was going to leave Jaden alive, so she squeezed the trigger on her gun and pumped a few more rounds into his body. She was sure that she hadn't missed her mark because his screams of pain filled her ears, right as she and Rich ran out of the house and to their car. Jaden had never been shot before and he wasn't sure that he was going to make it out alive. It was becoming harder for him to breathe and it felt like he was losing consciousness. He wanted to yell for his baby, but he was too weak to even do that. He wanted to stay up to let her know that he was okay, but it was a battle between darkness and light, and the dark was quickly gaining momentum. Jaden remembered his mother always telling him to pray, but he never listened. It was ironic that he wanted to do it now when it was possibly too late. Not being able to hold on any longer, Jaden closed his eyes and welcomed the darkness that so badly wanted to consume him.

Stay Tuned For The Conclusion of This Story... Coming Soon.

Made in the USA
Middletown, DE
06 August 2020